"It w[...]tend to

"No! No, that's not a good idea. I'm not good at...pretense. I won't be able to fool anyone."

"Listen, you don't have to worry." He was glad he could reassure her honestly. "I'm not going to take advantage of the situation. We may have to hold hands and look at each other all mushy-eyed in public, but leave that part to me." He grinned. "I can lust in my heart with the best of 'em. But trust me. That's where it will stay."

"Oh," she said in a small voice and, disappointed, she took the ring.

"I'll keep my hands to myself," he said, slowing as they neared the ferry that would take them to the island. "I promise."

Darn the man and his stupid promises!

Dear Reader,

All of us at Silhouette Desire send you our best wishes for a joyful holiday season. December brings six original, deeply touching love stories warm enough to melt your heart!

This month, bestselling author Cait London continues her beloved miniseries THE TALLCHIEFS with the story of MAN OF THE MONTH Nick Palladin in *The Perfect Fit*. This corporate cowboy's attempt to escape his family's matchmaking has him escorting a *Tallchief* down the aisle. Silhouette Desire welcomes the cross-line continuity FOLLOW THAT BABY to the line with Elizabeth Bevarly's *The Sheriff and the Impostor Bride*. And those irresistible bad-boy James brothers return in Cindy Gerard's *Marriage, Outlaw Style,* part of the OUTLAW HEARTS miniseries. When a headstrong bachelor and his brassy-but-beautiful childhood rival get stranded, they wind up in a 6lb., 12oz. bundle of trouble!

Talented author Susan Crosby's third book in THE LONE WOLVES miniseries, *His Ultimate Temptation,* will entrance you with this hero's primitive, unyielding desire to protect his once-wife and their willful daughter. A rich playboy sweeps a sensible heroine from her humdrum life in Shawna Delacorte's Cinderella story, *The Millionaire's Christmas Wish*. And Eileen Wilks weaves an emotional, edge-of-your-seat drama about a fierce cop and the delicate lady who poses as his newlywed bride in *Just a Little Bit Married?*

These poignant, sensuous books fill any Christmas stocking—and every reader's heart with the glow of holiday romance. Enjoy!

Best regards,
Joan Marlow Golan
Senior Editor

Please address questions and book requests to:
Silhouette Reader Service
U.S.: 3010 Walden Ave., P.O. Box 1325, Buffalo, NY 14269
Canadian: P.O. Box 609, Fort Erie, Ont. L2A 5X3

JUST A LITTLE BIT MARRIED?

EILEEN WILKS

SILHOUETTE *Desire*
Published by Silhouette Books
America's Publisher of Contemporary Romance

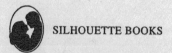

SILHOUETTE BOOKS

ISBN 0-373-76188-0

JUST A LITTLE BIT MARRIED?

Printed in U.S.A.

EILEEN WILKS

is a fifth-generation Texan. Her great-great-grandmother came to Texas in a covered wagon shortly after the end of the Civil War—excuse us, the War Between the States. But she's not a full-blooded Texan. Right after another war, her Texan father fell for a Yankee woman. This obviously mismatched pair proceeded to travel to nine cities in three countries in the first twenty years of their marriage, raising two kids and innumerable dogs and cats along the way. For the next twenty years they stayed put, back home in Texas again—and still together.

Eileen figures her professional career matches her nomadic upbringing, since she tried everything from drafting to a brief stint as a ranch hand—raising two children and any number of cats and dogs along the way. Not until she started writing did she "stay put," because that's when she knew she'd come home. Readers can write to her at P.O. Box 4612, Midland, TX 79704-4612.

This book is for all my buddies in the Romance Forum at Compuserve, and especially for Silke, Sherry and Bonnie, who helped with motorcycles, blood, bullets and other emergencies. Hi, guys!

One

He dreamed of snow and cold and blood.

Raz was naked when the phone rang that December morning. His covers lay on the floor where he'd kicked them at some point during the restless night. His skin was chilled, clammy, and he told himself that was why he'd dreamed of the cold again.

But he knew better. He knew what the cold meant, and where the blood had come from.

The phone rang again. He groped for it as he sat up. "Rasmussin," he muttered, reaching automatically for the cigarettes and lighter that should be right beside the phone. Then he remembered. He'd quit. Two months and three days and—he glanced at the clock—seven hours ago, he'd quit smoking. He cursed tiredly.

"Good morning to you, too," his brother said.

Raz rubbed a hand over his chest, where some of the cold from the dream seemed to be lodged. The warmth from his hand didn't dispel it. "It's seven-fifteen," he said irritably. "You want to know how much sleep I've had?"

"Not especially," Tom said. The slight hiss of static told Raz that Tom was on his cellular phone. "I want you to drag your lazy butt out of bed and listen. Javiero got to one of my witnesses last night. The orderly."

"Damn." Raz might not be on the H.P.D. payroll at the moment, but the habit of years was too strong to break. Houston was his city. He kept up with what happened in it, so he knew which case Tom was talking about. Three weeks ago bullets had filled a local emergency room when Javiero and two other members of the Padres "deposed" their current leader. Four people were killed, three others injured.

The press and the public dubbed it the worst outbreak of gang violence yet, perhaps because it happened on supposedly safe territory, away from the Padres' turf. Because of the uproar, the case had come to Tom in Special Investigations. Tom's task force had since caught up with the other two gunmen, but Javiero was still loose. "Is the orderly dead?"

"What do you think? Javiero went right to the guy's home with that Uzi of his. The bullets damn near cut my witness in half. The neighbor who was talking to him when the little bastard opened up is in critical condition."

"Damn." Reluctantly Raz faced the fact that he was wide awake at seven-fifteen in the morning and there were no cigarettes in the apartment. For the thousandth time he wondered why he'd picked this time to quit. "You have other witnesses."

"One of them suffered a severe loss of memory after he heard about the shooting last night."

"And the other?"

"She's sticking." There was satisfaction in Tom's voice. "Even though she's scared spitless, and with reason. I don't have the manpower to get her the kind of round-the-clock protection she needs until we catch up with Javiero."

An alarm went off in Raz's mind. "Tom, I don't—"

"I've persuaded her to hire a bodyguard. She's a doctor, so she can afford it."

"Fine. Great. Have you suggested North's agency? They're reliable."

"You claim you want to go private. Of course, we both know that's just an excuse to sit around in your underwear and watch your toenails grow. How many jobs have you turned down this month?"

Three. "I've been looking."

"How many have you turned down?"

"None of your goddamn business."

Silence from the other end, except for the muted sounds of traffic that indicated Tom was in his car.

"Look," Raz said, rubbing a hand over his face. Several days' worth of stubble rasped his palm. "I guess you mean well, but I don't need my big brother to ride in and save me from myself. I can find my own job." When he had to. When the right job turned up. He still had some money saved up, after all. There was no rush.

Tom snorted. "You really believe I'm thinking of you here? I don't risk my witnesses for you or anyone else. I need a guard for her. I want you to do it. When you're not busy feeling sorry for yourself, you're almost as good as you think you are."

"Private security companies—"

"They aren't good enough. Not for this."

Raz's eyebrows went up. Could his by-the-book brother actually have allowed himself to get personally involved in a case? Not with the witness, of course. Tom was too honorable to cheat on his wife. Besides, he was head-over-heels in love with her.

"I want you for it," Tom said flatly. "Jacy got a threatening note from Javiero yesterday. Apparently he doesn't like the coverage she's been giving his story."

Oh, sweet Jesus. "She's all right? And the baby?"

"Both of them are fine. She says I'm overreacting. A dozen

other journalists, both print and TV, got similar messages yesterday. Even a nutcase like Javiero can't go around killing them all, not when he's trying to hide out."

"It may be more of a power trip than a real threat."

"Has your brain rotted out completely in the last couple months? I take a death threat from a man who's killed at least five people pretty seriously."

Raz bit back his too-ready anger. Tom was entitled to be touchy under the circumstances. "Javiero is scum, but he's not stupid scum. By now he knows he's going down. He just wants to make it happen his way. Sending death threats to journalists gets him more press, more attention."

"If he really believed he was going down he wouldn't be offing witnesses."

Raz grimaced. Tom was one hell of a cop. The best. But he didn't understand Javiero. Raz did. He'd lived with people like that for years. Hell, he'd *been* someone like that, in one of his alter egos. "One thing you have to understand about Javiero. Death and prison don't worry him much, but pride, name, reputation—they mean everything. If he makes a big enough splash, takes enough people with him when he goes down, it makes him more real."

"Maybe," Tom said. "Maybe that is his motive right now—attention. He probably doesn't realize Jacy is my wife. She still uses her maiden name professionally. But once he finds out—if he finds out—his attitude is apt to change."

Raz's knuckles went white on the receiver. Tom was right. If Javiero found out that one of the reporters he'd threatened was the wife of the cop who was pursuing him, it might make an attack on her irresistible.

With Jacy in danger, Raz had no choice. He had to do whatever he could, even if that meant being responsible for this witness's life.

Even though the witness was a woman.

He took a deep breath and fought back the panic churning in his stomach. "What do you want me to do?"

"Take care of my witness. Keep her alive until we find Javiero and lock him up. I don't want that son of a bitch walking when this goes to trial."

"One witness's testimony is no guarantee of a conviction." Eyewitnesses were, in fact, notoriously unreliable.

"We've got physical and circumstantial evidence, too, but I need her. Juries don't always trust a lab tech's report, and this woman makes a hell of a good witness."

"Tell me about her."

"She's a doctor, a trauma specialist, though she doesn't look it. I doubt she's more than an inch over five foot, and—"

Raz interrupted impatiently. "I didn't ask for a physical description. What is she like?"

"Quiet. Intense. Easy to underestimate. She's got one hell of a memory for faces, fortunately, and when she's sure of her facts she can't be budged. She's sure it was Javiero she saw that night. She recognized him."

"How did she know him?"

"She volunteers at the free clinic on Burroughs twice a month. It seems he took his sister there a couple times."

"Sounds like a real saint."

"Just make sure she doesn't get changed from a saint into a martyr."

Raz promised. What else could he do? He knew what Tom was asking, knew *why* he was asking. Houston had several top-notch security agencies that could offer excellent round-the-clock protection, but professionals, however competent, weren't enough. Not when Jacy's life might be in danger.

Tom offered to call Raz's boss and get the paperwork started that would grant him official permission to work a civilian job while still technically on the force.

"I could just quit," Raz said.

"Not necessary," Tom said, as Raz had known he would, adding, "I'll be there to pick you up in ten minutes."

"Pretty sure of me, weren't you?" The hand that held the phone was starting to shake—a fine tremor, nothing obvious.

"Yes," Tom said quietly. "I'm sure of you."

More the fool you, Raz thought. He said goodbye and put the phone down. Then he waited for the shakes to pass.

Tom didn't understand what he was asking, not really. There was a hell of a lot Tom didn't know. But Raz understood what Tom wanted. He wanted someone who would keep his witness alive, no matter what.

Raz headed for the shower, wondering if Tom realized just how far his little brother would go to protect his family. Could a man as honest as Tom, a cop that straight arrow, imagine what Raz was really like after eight years of undercover work?

God, he hoped not.

The drumming of hot water on his back and head felt good, though it didn't banish the exhaustion that clung to him like a second skin. He didn't really notice, though. He'd been tired too long.

When he came out of the shower he flicked the radio on. A disc jockey announced there were only thirteen shopping days left until Christmas.

Raz stopped in his tracks, naked and dripping. Thirteen days? Only thirteen days until Christmas? Disbelieving, he looked out the window of his second-story apartment. A sunny South Texas sky promised another warm day.

He had vaguely noticed holiday decorations going up, but people put those up earlier every year. He hadn't paid attention to them. He hadn't wanted to see them at all. But surely they hadn't been up very long…had they?

The disk jockey's patter gave way to Bing Crosby singing about a white Christmas. Raz thought about the snow in his dream, shivered, and shut the radio off.

So Christmas was less than two weeks away. Christmas, the time of hope and miracles…and everything else Raz couldn't believe in anymore. But he did believe in family. If he had to lie, steal, kill or die to protect his family, that's what he'd do.

Though it was December, the air was barely cool that morning as a swimmer stroked up and down an outdoor pool in a

Houston neighborhood filled with old houses and new money.

The sun had been up for twenty minutes when Sara Grace finished her first lap. The water was cooler than the air, almost chilly. It flowed like liquid silk over her skin. Sara loved the feel of it as much as she liked the pull and warmth of her muscles as she stroked and kicked. Water was innately sensual. Here, for a little while, she could feel sensual, too. Here she was lithe and graceful and quite unlike her usual self.

As she slid through the water she let her mind slide into a daydream. It was better than thinking about what bullets, fired at a rate of 950 rounds per minute, could do to a human body. Like hers.

Sara had never had much time for daydreaming, so she wasn't very good at it. She vaguely imagined the feel of strong, male arms around her. The look of a man's hard, muscular body. A teasing flash of a smile. The combination brought a little tingle of excitement to her own body.

When she reached the south end of the pool she paused long enough to assure herself that the police officer still stood by the gate, watching over her. Then she flipped around and started back.

What had happened to the poor orderly last night had left her terrified. No surprise there. Sara knew she was a coward. But, being an experienced coward, she knew how to banish her fears, at least temporarily. Fear was an ice demon, tight and rigid. It had a hard time holding on to a body warm and loose from exercise. By the time she reached the other end of the pool she made her turn automatically, her mind drifting back to the man she'd been fantasizing about, a man she'd stitched up six months ago.

She'd been on her third night in a new job in a new city when he'd shown up at the ER. Sara remembered the number of stitches she'd put in the gash in the man's forearm, and she remembered the way his chest had looked—hard, with a dusting of soft brown hair in the center.

Once again she felt that pleasant little tingle of heat.

Her recently developed fantasy life was strangely soothing, rather like having a secret place to go when life became too large and scary. A bit childish, maybe, she thought, but it hurt no one. She did feel slightly guilty for drawing on her memory of a patient's anatomy for her daydreams. But he'd only been her patient for a couple of hours, after all. She'd never see him again.

Sara stroked smoothly down the length of the pool and thought about the man she would never see again. A dangerously attractive man—sexy, charming—oh, yes, he'd been all of that and more. More, as in possibly wanted by the police. He'd claimed the cut on his arm was an accident, but Sara knew a knife wound when she sewed one up. She'd reported it, of course. He'd sneaked out of the examining room before the officer came to get his statement.

Sara was nearly at the south end of the pool again when a man's voice interrupted her daydream. "Dr. Grace?"

Shock and fear jolted through her. Her head went up. Her hand, outstretched at the end of a stroke and ready to grab the side of the pool, froze. In that split second she saw not one, but two men. The detective she'd spoken with so often since the shooting knelt by the edge of the pool, his face shadowed by his black Stetson.

Behind him stood the man of her dreams.

Sara nearly drowned.

After several embarrassing seconds of splashing around like a two-year-old in a wading pool, she managed to grab the edge of the pool. She drew herself up with as much dignity as she could. "Yes?"

"Sorry," Lieutenant Rasmussin said in the Texas drawl Sara had almost gotten used to hearing in the past six months. He was a hard-looking man with a thick mustache and odd, pale eyes. "I didn't mean to startle you. I brought someone I'd like you to meet."

Her eyes flicked to the man behind him.

He reminded Sara of a young Harrison Ford, cocky and entirely too charming, his face intriguingly creased when he smiled. His jeans were faded almost to white. His T-shirt was a truly ugly shade of purple, covering a chest that surely couldn't be the peak of masculine perfection she remembered.

The crooked grin he flashed at her was the same, though. And, oh, heavens, she felt the same little sizzle of heat. Except it wasn't that little.

She cleared her throat. "We've met."

One of his eyebrows went up quizzically. "We have?"

It was absurd to feel disappointed. She wasn't a woman who made a lasting impression. And surely she hadn't wanted a man like him to be the exception? "I sewed up your arm a few months ago, Mr. MacReady."

His lips twitched. "Uh-oh." He glanced at the other man. "You were right about her memory for faces. She, uh, knows me as Eddie MacReady."

Lieutenant Rasmussin's expression barely changed, yet he managed to look disgusted. "You might have said something."

"I didn't know who your witness was. You've kept their names from the press, though God alone knows how."

"Apparently it didn't do much good, since Javiero found the other one." Tom Rasmussin sighed and stood. "Explanations are obviously in order. Dr. Grace, this reprobate is my brother, also known as Sergeant Ferdinand Rasmussin of the Houston Police Department. Also known by various other names, including Eddie MacReady. He works undercover and he has a sick sense of humor. Raz, meet Dr. Sara Grace."

She stared at the reprobate. He was a police officer? Now that she looked closely, she saw differences between her memory of him and the way he looked today. His clothes were vastly different, of course. This man's hair was shorter and lacked the blond highlights she remembered. And his eyes. There was something different about his eyes, but she couldn't pin down what it was.

He smiled at her, a smile as slow and as sweet as the choc-olate-candy color of those eyes. "Call me Raz," he said, look-ing almost bashful, as if he should have a hat to doff and boots to scuff in the dirt. "Glad to meet you under my right name this time, ma'am."

Detective Rasmussin scowled at his brother. "Stop playing around, Raz."

He shrugged. "I've got to do something to counter the im-pression she has of me. Eddie's not a very nice boy."

Sara was confused. On several levels. "You, ah, you want your brother to take over for the other officer?" she asked the detective. "You're assigning him to stay with me until I get a bodyguard?"

"Not exactly. Raz is on leave from the force right now. Do you want to get out and dry off, Dr. Grace, before I explain?"

Get out—in front of these two men—in her swimsuit?

Sara's face heated. Nerves fluttered in her stomach, and her throat closed. The rising tide of symptoms was only too fa-miliar, but no easier to combat because of it. She reminded herself that her swimsuit was a conservative one-piece. And these men didn't care what she looked like. They wouldn't be checking out her body for flaws. Besides, she'd look more ridiculous if she stayed in the pool.

But real shyness couldn't be reasoned away. She was barely able to stammer, "I'll, uh—my towel. It's—if you'd just—"

The wrong man figured out what her fractured request meant. The one she thought of as Eddie MacReady turned and grabbed her towel from the webbed chair where she'd left it. He crouched near the edge of the pool.

"Here." He smiled as he held out the towel.

This was awful. He was so close, and looking right at her. Sara shut her eyes and heaved herself up and out. She sat on the edge of the pool and twisted to take the towel from him, eager to get it wrapped safely around herself. Her fingers trem-bled slightly when they brushed his.

Heat. Quick. Purifying. It zipped through her in a sudden

rush. Just that fast, her shakes and sick nerves were gone, washed out by something stronger. Her hand clenched the towel. She stared at him, astonished.

His eyes were wide and startled and, for a split second, completely unguarded.

"Do you want to go in?" Lieutenant Rasmussin said.

His voice brought Sara back to reality. Partway back, at least, enough to realize she still sat there in her skin-hugging swimsuit. She blushed and hastily wrapped the thick terry towel around her. "Yes," she said, and pushed to her feet. "I'll fix coffee."

Now, of course, he would see what had been hidden by the water. But while Sara was painfully self-conscious about some things, she had her pride. She was proud of the fact that she walked at all, and damned if she would be ashamed of the scars.

Her back was straight even if her gait couldn't be when she limped to the chair where she'd left her cane. She started for her cottage then, and she didn't look back.

Two

"**W**hy didn't you tell me?" Raz demanded in a low voice. The sound of the shower his subject was taking traveled clearly through the wall to where he and his brother stood in the kitchen of her dollhouse-sized cottage.

Sara Grace lived on Highpoint Avenue—typical doctor territory, expensive and exclusive. She rented from a doctor, in fact—the chief of surgery at her hospital. But Sara's home was a tiny "mother-in-law" house built behind the mansion by a previous owner. Her kitchen was a narrow, unfussy room with several plants hung in front of the long window in lieu of curtains. Like the rest of the house, it had wooden floors. A basket in the center of the table held a miniature holly bush covered with red berries and tiny red bows. Beneath it was a red place mat with a holiday border.

Christmas. Now that Raz had noticed the holiday, he saw it everywhere.

The coffeemaker that sat at one end of the green-and-white-tiled counter gave a last burp and gurgle. Tom set his hat on the counter and reached for the pot. "Tell you what?"

"That she was injured when Javiero went gunning for his rival at the emergency room." Damn, he felt edgy. Automatically he patted his pocket, then pulled his hand away when he remembered. No cigarettes.

"She wasn't. I don't know why she limps, but it's not from the shooting. Want a cup?"

"Yeah." He moved restlessly around her small kitchen, trying to get a handle on the woman he was supposed to keep alive. Dr. Sara Grace—physician, trauma specialist, witness...and a pretty, frightened mouse with a bad leg.

Seeing her limp had bothered Raz. He didn't know why. It didn't seem to be a severe handicap. She'd walked almost normally once she had the cane to help. Maybe it was the contrast. She'd been so at home in the pool, a sleek water creature, small and strong and sure.

He thought of his reaction to her once she left that water. Amusement, dark and supple, twisted in him.

"Care to share the joke?" his brother asked, handing him a steaming mug.

"Not really." Raz sipped. The coffee was one of those fancy gourmet brands, the first evidence of extravagance he'd seen in Sara Grace's life-style. "I've got some questions to ask before she rejoins us," Raz said.

"Go ahead."

"What kind of back-up have I got?"

"I can have someone here eight hours out of twenty-four."

"Wait a minute." He frowned. "You said 'here.' Don't you have a safe house lined up for her?"

"She won't go."

"Won't go?" Raz's eyebrow went up. "She didn't strike me as stupid."

"Feel free to try and talk her out of staying here."

He would. Not only was this cottage of hers unsafe from a professional standpoint, it was *small*. He'd be bumping into her every time either of them turned around, and he did not need the distraction. Not when he'd already experienced the most extraordinary burst of lust for her trim little body.

Lusting after his subject was certainly not a complication

he'd expected to have to deal with. Never mind whether he deserved that particular frustration or not. Life had little to do with people getting what they deserved. "You've pointed out to her that if she recognized Javiero, he must have seen her, too?"

Tom shrugged and sipped his coffee. His mug was white with a cartoon reindeer on the front. "Most people don't have her memory for faces. She's gambling that he didn't remember her."

"Funny. She doesn't look like a gambler." But Raz had to admit that he hadn't recognized her, either, and he was trained to remember faces. Of course, he'd been halfway drunk the night she stitched up his arm. "I thought you said she was scared stiff."

A faint sound made him turn.

Sara Grace stood in the doorway, her pointy chin lifted, her eyes a soft, serious, blue-gray. "I am scared, but I'm not running away."

Dry, she looked more mouselike than ever. She was so *little*. Her hair was cut very short and framed her face in a dark, feathery fringe. Her olive-toned skin probably should have made him think of the Mediterranean, but instead he was reminded of the tawny color of the field mice he'd kept in a shoe box in his closet when he was ten...until they had babies and his mother found out.

He smiled. "That's an admirable attitude, but not very sensible under the circumstances."

"I'm always sensible." Her voice was Southern-belle soft, but her accent was pure, clipped Yankee. It was a strangely appealing combination.

"Then you'll go to a safe house."

"No. I have a job to do."

He shook his head. It bothered him that he couldn't remember her. He was used to relying on his memory for people. But she didn't *look* like a doctor, much less one who specialized in the bloody drama of a hospital emergency room. Her eyes were too big and innocent. Her clothes were just too big.

"No one is indispensable," he told her Her pants were

baggy khakis. Her white shirt was so loose it hid the existence of her breasts entirely, but he'd seen her in a swimsuit. He remembered their shape, small and firm, nicely molded in powder-blue Lycra right down to the hard little nipples. "No one is indispensable. The hospital can do without you for a few days while Tom gets this straightened out."

"It might be more than a few days, though, mightn't it? And you're wrong. In the ER, the presence or absence of key personnel can be the difference between life and death."

"Your presence will make a big difference, all right, if Javiero comes after you while you're at work."

"He wouldn't—"

"He did once, didn't he? That's how this all started. He'd already tangled with his rival once that night, and when the man came to your emergency room to get his ribs taped up, Javiero followed with his Uzi."

She shook her head. "That's not what I mean. I mean that he's more apt to come after me here, at home. Security has been stepped up so much at the hospital. There's no reason for him to—to make things hard on himself. Anyway, I doubt very much he knows who I am."

"You're willing to risk people's lives based on your assessment of the situation?"

"I risk people's lives based on my assessment of their situation every day."

Raz ran a hand through his hair. He couldn't picture it. He just couldn't picture this soft little creature cracking a man's rib cage so she could get to his heart. "You mean you use your professional judgment every day. Why won't you trust ours?"

"I'm sorry," she said in that deceptively soft voice. "The hospital is already short on staff. I'm needed there. But..." She paused. "If Detective Rasmussin finds evidence that indicates Javiero does know my identity, I'll reconsider."

God, she was stubborn. And he was getting hard, for no reason at all. His reaction infuriated him. "You won't be able to do your job with a couple dozen slugs in you."

Her pale cheeks turned paler. "If you and the other officers do *your* job, that won't happen, will it?"

Tom broke in. "Raz won't be working with the other officers, Dr. Grace. As I said, I can't assign you round-the-clock protection. I know you weren't very happy at the idea of hiring a bodyguard—"

"I'm not." Two faint spots of embarrassed color appeared on her cheeks. "Excuse me. I didn't mean to interrupt."

"No problem. Like I was saying, I know you aren't crazy about having a bodyguard underfoot all the time. That's why I brought Raz to meet you. He's on leave right now, so he could take a private job."

She looked at Tom in disbelief. "You mean—you mean you want me to hire *him?*"

"Hey," Raz protested. "I'm not so bad. Honest."

Tom shot him a look that told him to keep his big mouth shut, then said to her, "Would you like me to pour you a cup of your coffee while we talk about this? It's pretty good stuff compared to what I get down at headquarters."

She smiled shyly and, at last, moved into the room. "Please. And refill your own cup, too, if you like."

So, Raz thought, Sara Grace might argue with him, but she smiled at his brother. It was supposed to be the other way around. Women generally liked Raz, while Tom made them nervous.

He noticed something else, too. "You don't need to use your cane all the time?"

She shot a quick, surprised glance his way and paused near the table. "I don't have to use it at all. It just helps, especially if my hip's sore. The ER was busy last night, so I was on my feet a lot."

So the problem was with her hip, not her leg. "I guess you were at work when Tom told you about the other witness. The one Javiero shredded last night." He wanted her to face the reality of what she risked with her refusal to go to a safe house.

"As it happens, I was on duty when they brought his body in."

Raz felt foolish. For a moment he couldn't think of anything to say. Belatedly, his mother's training came to his rescue. He pulled out one of the ladder-back chairs and held it for her.

Now she looked at him—a suspicious look, as if she thought he might jerk the chair out from under her as soon as she tried to sit down.

He shook his head, torn between amusement and chagrin. "Sit down and we'll talk," he said, offering her one of his best guy-next-door grins. "You can point out some of my shortcomings and I'll listen, then I'll try to persuade you to hire me, anyway. I'll promise not to pounce if you will, too."

She blushed. With color staining her cheeks she was as helplessly charming as a three-week-old kitten or a dandelion puff. Raz looked at soft skin flushed in a delightful mimicry of arousal, and a beast woke inside him. A selfish, hungry, very male beast.

He forgot to keep smiling. Fortunately, she'd turned away to sit in the chair he held. He slid it in under her. When he took the seat at right angles to hers he had to adjust his jeans to accommodate the effect she had on him.

Life was sure as hell ironic at times.

Tom brought her a mug of coffee—this one in bright red with a Santa on the front—sat, and began talking about bodyguards in general and Raz's qualifications in particular. Raz listened to his brother make him sound like the best thing to come along since color TV and fought the urge to get up and walk out.

When Tom finished, Sara nodded and turned those big, serious eyes on Raz. Her fingers toyed nervously with the fringe of hair at her nape. "Sergeant Rasmussin—"

"Make it Raz," he interrupted, smiling.

"Raz, then. I'd like to know why you're on leave."

"I'm considering leaving the department permanently." He'd had to give this explanation several times lately, so it flowed easily enough. "A couple of people talked me into taking unpaid leave instead of resigning outright, while I mull things over. I could use some income while I'm mulling."

"I see." She turned back to Tom. "I hope you'll forgive

my saying this, but it strikes me as odd that you would propose
your brother for this job.''

"It's damned irregular," Tom said bluntly. "You probably
should know my reasons."

Sara listened with increasing dismay as she heard about the
threat to the detective's wife. He told her he'd recommended
his brother for her bodyguard because "the suspect's actions
have introduced a personal element to the case." He added
that Raz might be irritating, but he was very, very good. Under
the circumstances, that was what he wanted for her.

It isn't fair. It just isn't fair at all. Sara bit her lip when she
heard that old refrain singing in her head. Hadn't she gotten
over that attitude years and years ago, when she put the accident behind her and got on with her life? Yet that was her
first reaction when she felt herself caving in to the pressure
the two men were putting on her.

Surely hiring this man would be a bad idea. He made her—
well—*hot.* And bothered. And mortified. The reactions met
and clashed every time she looked at him.

But Detective Rasmussin's wife was in danger. He deserved
to have some peace of mind about that, didn't he? And she
liked looking at the detective's brother. In spite of her confusion of responses, she liked it very much.

Sara sneaked another glance at the gorgeous man sitting
next to her, right there in her kitchen. He'd never notice her,
that was certain, but did it really hurt for her to have him
around to look at?

Dumb, Sara. Very dumb. She shook her head. "I don't think
so."

"How about giving me a test drive?" the man with the
candy-colored eyes asked in a voice that could coax birds from
the trees. "You haven't hired anyone yet. Keep me around
while you consider your options."

It made sense. It made too much sense, and she was weak-
ening. "We haven't discussed money."

Five minutes later she'd handed over the extra key to her
front door. He was hired on a trial basis only, she reminded
all of them, feeling breathless from the speed with which she'd

capitulated. He agreed—and a minute later, his brother put on his hat and left.

And she was alone with the object of her sexual fantasies.

Sara knew exactly how to deal with the situation. She murmured a few words about taking a nap—at 8:45 in the morning—and fled to her bedroom.

She certainly didn't expect him to follow her.

"Dr. Grace?" he called through the door.

She looked around, as if her bedroom might have sprouted another exit overnight. But unless she was willing to climb out one of the two high windows along the back wall, she was trapped in a room that revealed too much about a part of herself she preferred to keep private. The romantic part.

Sara had never had a house all to herself before, not even a little house like this one. When she moved down here she'd gone a bit crazy in decorating her bedroom, which was the largest room in the cottage. She'd used scarves and gauze and lace in dreamy colors. Her bed was much too big for one person and mounded with pillows. She sat on her ridiculously big bed now and clutched a mint green pillow to her chest.

No way would she suggest he open that door. "Yes?"

"I understand you're used to sleeping days since you work nights, and that will work out fine with me. I've worked nights more than days myself. But I have to leave for a little while."

Her relief was enormous. "Oh?"

"I need to bring some of my things over here."

Oh. Bring his things over here. That sounded so...definite. Her voice was thin when she answered. "I'll see you later, then." At least he'd be gone long enough for her to put some cat food down for the tomcat she'd been trying to befriend the past three weeks.

She did *not* want this man to learn what she'd named that ungrateful cat.

"Don't worry," he said, reassuring her for the wrong thing. "Officer Palmer will be right outside until I get back, and I won't be gone more than an hour. Stay inside until then, okay?"

An hour was a pathetically short time for a woman like her

to adjust to living with a man like him. Sara sighed. "I seldom leave the apartment when I'm asleep."

He chuckled. "I guess not. Later, when you're awake, we'll need to go over some ground rules."

Ground rules?

She straightened. Maybe he thought he was going to be the one making those rules, but she had her own ideas about that. "That sounds like a very good idea, Sergeant."

"Raz," he corrected her. "See you soon, Sara."

When Raz pulled out of the long driveway that led past the big, colonial-style house, he was satisfied that things were going to go his way.

First, of course, he had to persuade her not to go in to work until Javiero was found and locked up. Sara Grace had shown herself to be surprisingly stubborn about going to a safe house, but then, she was a dedicated woman. A saint.

A susceptible saint. Susceptible to him, anyway. Raz acknowledged it without ego or pleasure as he headed for his apartment. It had been obvious, once he'd set out to charm her into agreeing to hire him, that he would succeed.

The pretty little mouse wanted him. Poor baby.

He would use that. He was guilty of so much worse that using Sara Grace's unwilling attraction to him to help him prolong her life wouldn't bother him at all.

Sara didn't try to sleep. As soon as Raz left she went to the kitchen, filled a plastic bowl with dry cat food and carried it to the front porch.

Standing on her own porch wasn't exactly leaving the house, she assured herself. Technically speaking she was still beneath her own roof, which extended out over the porch, and she had walls on two sides, so she wasn't really exposed. And she could see the police officer standing guard at the gate. He obviously hadn't seen Javiero creeping up on her. So she was safe enough.

Because she didn't want the policeman to hear, she called very softly, "MacReady? Breakfast time." She set the bowl down, looked around and called a bit louder. "Mac? Here, kitty-kitty!"

There was no sign of the ornery cat she'd named for her new bodyguard's alter ego. Sara sighed. So far Houston had proved a bit lonely. She'd expected that when she'd made the decision to move here. After all, her social skills were barely up to befriending a starving alley cat. Making human friends was going to take time.

Unconsciously Sara began to toy with the hair at the back of her neck, a habit she had when she was troubled. Maybe it was the nearness of the holiday that made her feel the loneliness more keenly. Sometimes lately she even missed her aunt.

How ridiculous. In most of the ways that counted, Aunt Julia was no more distant now than she had been for years. They talked on the phone once a month, just as they had when they lived thirty miles apart instead of a thousand. Even if Sara had still been living in Connecticut, she could only have counted on receiving a box through the mail with a Christmas present or two in it, rather than an invitation to spend the holiday together. Aunt Julia craved solitude the way most people craved the company of their fellows.

Sara shook her head to dispel the maudlin mood. Hadn't she learned to value her aunt for what she was instead of fretting over all that she wasn't? The box with the present or two hadn't arrived yet, but she knew it would. Her aunt might be distant, but she was as dependable, in her way, as the seasons.

Back inside, she went straight to the stereo and put on a couple of Christmas CDs, cranking the volume up before she headed for the kitchen. She hummed along with the London Boys' Choir while she assembled ingredients. It was only Tuesday, but she wasn't waiting for her usual baking day. She needed the exertion of kneading, the lusty scent of yeast and the satisfaction of creation to settle her mind.

Raz heard the music before he stepped onto the porch. He'd made a circuit of the outside of the little house, checking for ease of access, before talking with the cop on duty. Officer Palmer had informed him that the subject had stepped out onto the porch for a while.

Apparently she wasn't taking her situation seriously. Raz used the key she'd given him and walked into a room that all but shook from the chorus to Handel's *Messiah.*

Good Lord, didn't the woman have any sense? All forty or so of Javiero's old gang could break in and she'd never notice until they shot her down. He shook his head. People never failed to surprise him. Handel, now—that was just the sort of music he'd expect the little mouse to enjoy. But not at these decibels.

Her living room fit his image of her, though, and added to the impression the cottage gave of being a dollhouse. It was a tidy, feminine room, maybe ten feet square. The end table, bookcase and armchair were white wicker, and the print on the chair cushions and love seat was a dainty floral. A multitude of ornaments all but buried the small flocked Christmas tree in one corner.

Christmas again. He grimaced and studied the love seat pessimistically. It didn't look like it made out into a bed. They were going to have to have a talk about the sleeping arrangements. Among other things.

He set his garment bag down on the love seat but kept his shoulder holster in his hand when he went to her bookshelf. It shouldn't have surprised him to see it stuffed with medical books and back issues from magazines like the *New England Medical Journal,* but the grim realism of her reading material seemed incongruous in the dainty setting.

The bottom shelf of the bookcase held her stereo and one of those cordless phones that had an answering machine in the base unit and caller ID in the receiver. The caller ID was a sensible idea for a woman who lived alone. Yes, he thought, kneeling, Dr. Grace was a very sensible woman. In most ways.

He shut the stereo off, and silence dropped like a stone.

In the kitchen Sara froze. *Someone is here. Here, in the house.*

Fear swept through her, a cold fire that lit every cell, sending her heart rate skidding crazily. A series of images exploded in her head—images of bodies jerking with the peculiar rhythm of gunfire. She saw liquid red blossoms flowering around entry holes in chests, abdomens, elsewhere. She saw the surprised eyes of the security guard who'd shown her pictures of his grandchildren one evening. He'd slid to the floor so slowly, leaving a shiny red smear on the wall behind him.

And the noise. She heard it again, the terrible thunder of gunfire, a sound she heard often in her dreams and tried to drown out when awake.

Trembling, she pulled her hands out of the sticky bread dough she'd been kneading. The back door lay directly opposite the hall doorway. She took a step toward it.

A floorboard creaked in the hall.

She whirled, jerked a knife from the wooden block that held them on the counter behind her and turned back to face the intruder.

Raz walked into the kitchen.

Relief spread as quickly as fear had, leaving weakness behind. Her fingers lost their grip on the knife. It clattered to the floor.

"Oh," she said stupidly. "Oh, it's you."

His quick glance took in her white face and shaking hands, the knife on the floor. "Hey, I'm sorry," he said, coming toward her. "I didn't mean to—"

Sara didn't decide to scoop up a handful of dough and sling it at him. She just did it.

He stopped. He looked down, amazed, at the sticky dough slowly sliding down his chest. Then he looked at her.

"Are you crazy?" she demanded. "What's the matter with you?"

"Ah—I'm not the one throwing things around here." A smile tugged at his lips as most of the glob of dough splatted on the floor.

That smile made her even more angry. "Did you think I hired you to terrify me? Do I look like someone who wants to be terrified?"

"No," he said soothingly. "Not at all. You look like someone who wants to throw things at me. I'm just glad you dropped the knife first.''

The knife. Oh, God, what if she'd—? Sara's knees suddenly refused to hold her. She sank into the nearest chair. "I wouldn't have," she said. "I wouldn't have thrown it." Would she have used it at all, if he had been Javiero? Could she?

"Of course not." He came and knelt in front of her. She noticed vaguely that he held a leather belt in one hand. He set it on the floor beside him. "Are you okay?"

She shook her head, bewildered by herself. "I don't get mad. Not like that. At least," she added conscientiously, "not when there isn't a patient involved."

"But it's a natural reaction, to go from fear to fury. You're the doctor," he pointed out. "You ought to know about that sort of thing."

With him kneeling and her sitting, his face was slightly below hers. He smiled up at her with eyes the color of candy kisses and lips just as sweet. Sara felt the oddest fluttering in her middle, as if she'd swallowed a bird and it was trying to get out.

Right now, right this minute, he didn't look like Eddie MacReady at all. Neither did he look like the cocky police officer she'd met earlier. He looked…nice. As if he cared.

She flushed. *Stupid, Sara,* she told herself. His concern might be genuine, but was hardly personal. "I'm all right," she said, and started to smooth her hands on her slacks. She stopped just before she smeared dough all over herself.

He grinned, picked up the leather belt, and stood. "Well, I'm not. I think I'd better change before we have our talk. But first I really do need to apologize. I should have said something the second I turned the stereo off."

That wasn't a belt he carried, she realized. It was a shoulder holster. She saw the handle of the gun it carried. She swallowed, staring at the dull gray metal. "Why didn't you?"

He shrugged. "You were expecting me back about now, and so far you've seemed pretty oblivious to the danger you're in. It didn't occur to me you'd think someone had broken in."

"If that's another attempt to make me change my mind about the safe house, please don't."

"I didn't mean it that way, but I haven't given up." His smile this time held conscious charm—which made it all the more irritating when the fluttering started again inside her. "Tell you what. Rule number one—I might try to change your mind, but I'll let you know up front that's what I'm doing. Now, why don't I go change before I get any more dough on your floor?"

"The bathroom is right across from the kitchen." Sara felt unsteady and vaguely nauseous. She clasped her hands tightly together to keep them from shaking. Adrenaline was great stuff if you had to fight or flee, she reflected, but it played havoc with your system if you didn't get it all burned up.

"I'll be back in a few minutes," he said, "and we'll talk."

Sara didn't watch him leave the room. She forced herself to stand and go back to her dough.

She wasn't disappointed, she told herself as she kneaded, working off the lingering effects of the adrenaline, that Raz thought he could talk her into doing things his way. People often thought that because she was shy, she was a pushover. And she was, about some things.

Not about her profession.

She was needed at Memorial. With all the increased security at the hospital since the shooting, she should be just fine while she was there. It was later, when she was home again, that worried her.

Home…with her new bodyguard.

Three

Raz buckled his shoulder holster in place over a clean T-shirt. Damned if he'd put a jacket on just so she wouldn't have to look at his gun. He wasn't in the mood for tact. He'd seen the shocked look she'd given his weapon.

How had she thought he was going to protect her? Insults at fifty yards? Bad breath?

The rich smell of yeast filled the kitchen when he walked in. His subject stood at the table, wrist-deep in dough. She didn't look up.

At least this time she didn't turn deathly pale.

Raz was still shaken by what had happened earlier. His fault. Completely, stupidly his fault. He hadn't stopped to think, a sin for which there was no excuse. He couldn't even allow himself the luxury of confession. Admitting to her how thoroughly he'd messed up would only make her lose what little confidence she had in him, and that was more dangerous than his own doubts.

She glanced over at him. "Surely," she said, "you don't need to wear that—that holster of yours inside."

"The word is *gun*," he said, "and it won't do me much good if it's in one room and I'm in another." He knew what bothered her. Guns belonged to another world, a big, messy world that shouldn't be allowed to intrude on her here.

A world Raz knew only too well. "Baking bread?" he asked.

"No," she said shortly, turning back to her dough. "I'm kneading it. The baking comes later."

He grinned, more pleased by the touch of sarcasm than not. She looked very tidy and domestic standing there with her sleeves neatly rolled up, not one hair on her head out of place. Except...his grin widened. "You've got dough on the tip of your nose."

She lifted a hand automatically to wipe her nose, saw the dough covering it, and grimaced. "I suppose you want to have that talk you keep referring to," she said stiffly. "There's coffee, if you like. Or some fruit juice in the refrigerator."

"Juice sounds good." But instead of going to the refrigerator he stopped next to her. She glanced at him, wary. He reached out and skimmed a finger down her nose. Kind of a cute little nose, short and pointy. Her skin felt soft and fine pored, slightly cool, and made him think of thick cream.

She stared at him, suspicious and stirred. Such big eyes she had, the color of sky hazed by high-flying cirrus clouds. He liked looking into them almost as much as he liked touching her.

Too much.

He quickly rubbed the bit of dough off the tip of her nose and stepped back. Absurdly, his heart was pounding. He was sure—almost sure—his sudden turmoil didn't show. "There," he said, and wiped his hand on the towel that sat on the table before continuing to the refrigerator. "First a question. How bad is your hip?"

She blinked at him, startled. "Why do you ask?"

"If I tell you to run, can you?"

"Oh." She lifted half the dough, turned it, punched it down. "It depends. My hip wouldn't keep me from running, actually, though I'd probably be a bit awkward and slow. But the sciatic nerve damage that occurred when the joint was displaced affected my calf muscles. The degree of disability varies, depending on how tired the muscles are. Sometimes I hardly notice a problem. Sometimes…the muscles just don't cooperate.''

"Does that mean I shouldn't count on you being able to run?''

"If I've been using my cane, assume I can't run. If I haven't been using it, I could probably run for a couple blocks.''

"Good enough.'' He pulled out the clear pitcher that held an orangey-red juice. "Next question.'' He smiled. "Where are the glasses?''

"In the cabinet behind me.''

He closed the refrigerator. "Now tell me something else. Why are you so blasted certain you don't need to go to a safe house?''

She didn't look up. Her long, narrow hands looked surprisingly strong as they worked the dough rhythmically: lift, turn, press. "You answer a question for me first,'' she said at last. "How do you think Javiero found out where Carl lived?''

"There's no way to say for sure.''

"Give me your best guess.''

He stopped barely a foot away from her to open the cabinet and take out a glass. Beneath the ripe scent of the yeast he caught the freshness of flowers. He thought of the scented body lotion he'd seen in her bathroom and wondered where on her body he might find that very feminine scent. "The most likely way would be if he knew who Carl was from the first shooting, watched for him at the hospital, and followed him home.''

"That would indicate he doesn't want to risk the increased security at the hospital, wouldn't it? And that he doesn't have access to any special information about the witnesses' identities or addresses. And you,'' she said—lift, turn, press—"are supposed to see to it he doesn't follow me home.''

Damn. She was bright enough to be dangerous. "True,'' he agreed, pouring some juice. Her head was bent over her work, leaving the back of her neck bare except for a feathery fringe.

What would she say if he asked if he could put his face up against the delicate skin there so he could smell her better?

He shook his head, aggravated with himself. "But that's just the most likely explanation, not the only one. And he could change his mind about hospital security. Men like Javiero aren't gifted with patience."

"He hasn't had time to grow frustrated yet, and your brother's task force could pick him up any day." The dough grew supple and shiny as she continued to work it. "And Javiero is an inner-city gang member, not some criminal genius. How would he know how to find me? I'm pretty sure he didn't notice me that night."

"The night he brought his Uzi to the emergency room, you mean."

She nodded.

Raz leaned against the counter and considered the woman standing in front of him, kneading her bread dough. The juice was some exotic, tropical blend, not what he'd expected of her. But Sara Grace kept surprising him, didn't she?

She was frightened. He was sure of that. She'd been terrified earlier, and she was still afraid. But she was more stubborn than she was scared.

She irritated the hell out of him.

One way or another he had to take control back. Of himself and of her, too, since she refused to do what she should to keep herself safe. She had to be kept safe. He couldn't allow anything else.

The most powerful stimuli for humans were the same as those for other animals: hunger, fear and sex. He couldn't starve the blasted woman into submission, and fear had oddly little effect. So... "You know," he said, and smiled, "living together like this will be easier if we get to know each other a bit better."

"I...suppose so." Lift, turn, press.

He set down his juice and moved closer. Too close, by a couple inches, for courtesy. "I do have one other question." He could smell the flowers on her skin much better from here. He bent his head slightly.

Her voice was a touch breathless. "Oh?"

"Mmm-hmm." He watched the nervous color seep into her cheeks and eased even closer, wanting her to have his scent in her nostrils, too. Wanting her to react. "Where am I supposed to sleep?"

Her head stayed bent. The tip of her tongue darted out, touched her lips, then hid inside her mouth again. "I...I thought I might rent one of those beds. You know. The kind that folds up."

"Oh, yeah, I know what you mean." *And I know what you want, even if you aren't sure. Not sex, not yet, anyway. She wanted touching.* Raz reached up ever so casually to toy with that fringe of hair at her nape.

She jolted.

"Where should we put it?" His fingers skimmed her skin.

"Wh-what?" *Lift, turn, press. The dough was glossy and smooth now.*

"My bed." He pulled softly on one strand of hair. *Sweet Sara. She obviously knew she should say something, do something, but he kept his touch so light, so—nearly—innocent. She didn't know how to tell him to stop.*

Not when she liked it so much.

"In the living room, I guess," she managed.

"Do you think it will fit?" He smiled, enjoying his double meaning.

"I don't..." Her voice trailed off. Goose bumps appeared on her skin. She folded the dough over one more time, but this time she didn't squish it down. "I hadn't thought about it. I suppose it will...fit."

"That's good, then," he said softly. "In the living room will be fine." *Yes, in the living room would be good. He had a quick flash of Sara lying, stark naked, on that cramped little love seat with the pink and blue flowers. She was lifting her arms, welcoming him. Her legs were already parted.*

Somehow he didn't groan.

The look she slid him was wary, but her cheeks were pleasured pink from his attention. "I'm not—I need to—excuse me."

"You're excused," he said amiably, not moving. The fingers of his other hand, the one not touching her, curled into his palm. He wondered if her nipples were hard beneath that blasted shirt.

He was certainly hard, dammit.

"The dough," she said desperately. "It's ready to go in the bowl. Please move."

He stepped back, smiling and aching. "Sure."

She picked up the huge, yellow pottery bowl that sat next to her work space. She had to walk past him to carry it to the sink. He didn't move back quite far enough. She managed—barely—to get by without brushing against him.

Her cheeks were an even brighter pink as she ran water in the bowl.

He smiled at her back. "Why are you doing that?"

Her voice was almost inaudible over the running water. "I'm warming it up. The dough is supposed to stay quite warm from now on."

"So it will rise?" he asked innocently. "Heat makes it rise?"

She nodded and shut the water off.

When she moved past him again carrying the warmed bowl, her arm brushed against his. The innocent touch sent a current sweeping through him, a sizzling sexual charge all out of proportion to the action. He gritted his teeth against the absurd pull her slight body had on his. *This had better be working on her as well as it is on me.* "You know, it occurs to me this must be a bit awkward for you, having me suddenly living with you. I'm practically a stranger."

She darted him one quick, uneasy look and said nothing, lifting the heavy mass of dough in both hands.

"I know a few things about you, from having seen your house. You like to make bread, you listen to Christmas music too loud and you watch TV in bed."

Her eyes widened. "How did you know that?"

"Hey, I'm good at detecting. No television in the living room means that either you don't watch it, or that it's in your bedroom. I took a guess."

She laid the dough carefully in the bowl, seamed side down. A platter went upside down on top of the bowl. "Good guess."

"Why don't we eat out tonight? We can talk awhile, get to know each other. Maybe take in a movie." A movie was a great idea, in fact. As long as they weren't followed, they'd be much safer there than here.

She froze, her hands on each side of the yellow bowl. "I have to work."

"You know I don't think that's a good idea. That bowl looks heavy. Let me."

She shook her head. "I can get it. I always do."

As soon as she picked the bowl up he reached out. He ran his fingertips along the backs of her hands before gripping the bowl, his eyes fixed on hers the whole time. But she didn't let go.

Such a soft, drowning blue he looked into—such a mixture of confusion and desire. "You know," he said, not moving, "I really wish you'd consider taking a few days off from work."

Those eyes closed briefly. "Don't," she said, her voice strained. "Please don't."

"Don't what?" he challenged her softly.

Her eyes opened. The hurt in them condemned him as thoroughly as only real innocence could have done. "Rule number one, remember? You said you'd let me know when you were trying to change my mind."

Slowly he released his hold and stepped back. "There's something you may as well know about me, Sara Grace. I'm a very good liar."

She turned her back on him and walked over to the stove.

He let her settle her burden in the oven herself. The heavy silence between them was as painful, in its way, as the continued throbbing in his loins. And just as useless.

Poor mouse. She didn't know how little she really had to fear from him.

She closed the oven door and straightened. "I don't like being manipulated," she said.

He sent both eyebrows up. "I don't like being asked to risk my life by someone who's unwilling to trust me professionally."

She bit her lip. "I'm not—"

"Yes," he said, coming toward her. "You are. Remember Carl's neighbor? How many bullets did he take for being nearby when Javiero caught up with him?"

She flinched. "All right. All right. I guess I am, but that doesn't make it right for you to—to try to change my mind the way you did." Her chin came up. "I could fire you."

"You could." He stopped directly in front of her, close enough that she had to tilt her head back to continue to meet his eyes—which she did, though he could see it cost her. "But I don't think you will. You're too smart. Smart enough to be scared. Smart enough to know you can't hire the kind of devoted attention I'm going to give you while I'm your bodyguard. I'll tell you something else about me—"

"In addition to the fact that you're a liar?" she asked, two patches of color flaring on her cheeks.

"Yeah. In addition to that. Remember this—I'd do anything for my family. Which means I'll do anything I have to in order to keep you alive." He shook his head. "You don't want to fire me, Sara."

Now her eyes dropped. A long, silent moment later she spoke. "I'm going to take a nap. We'll talk about it when I wake up."

"That's fine," he said, knowing she wouldn't fire him, knowing he'd both won and lost. And he hated himself for his methods, but whether on her behalf, or his own, he wasn't sure. "You go right ahead. I'll be right here when you wake up."

He knew, of course, that was what she was afraid of.

What if he was right?

Sara lay on her bed, a pale green afghan snuggled up under her chin, and wished she could sleep instead of chasing her thoughts like a weary cat trying to catch a whole family of mice.

What if she were endangering others by insisting on going in to work? She honestly didn't think so, but *he* certainly seemed to think there was a danger. Sara lay quietly and tried to focus on what had to be the most important issue, but those little mice scurried all over the place.

Very few people ever commented directly on her limp. Her new bodyguard had referred to it as casually as he might have mentioned her height or hair color. His attitude had disconcerted her as much as it pleased her. Of course, he'd needed the information professionally. In case she needed to run for her life.

He knew his business, knew what to plan for. What if he was right about her going in to work? Was she exaggerating her own importance in the ER? Dr. Retger, her boss, had encouraged her to come in to work as usual, but Dr. Retger's specialty was trauma, not security. Maybe, she thought, rolling over restlessly onto her side, she should talk with Dr. Retger again.

But she'd go crazy, staying out of work for days and days—spending all day, all night, every day and night with *him*.

What would she have done if he'd gone on touching her? What if he'd actually wanted to touch her, the way those melted-chocolate eyes of his had claimed?

She wiggled over onto her stomach. How ridiculous. He'd been using his charm and her foolishness to get what he wanted from her, and what he wanted wasn't sex. The back of her throat still burned with humiliation, yet she didn't wholly blame him. He had family involved, after all. His brother's wife had been threatened. She thought it must be rather wonderful to have family who meant that much to you.

And what would it be like to mean that much to someone?

That thought brought her up sharply, as if she teetered on the edge of some chasm. A wind, dark and cold, swirled up from the empty depths, and the threat of it nearly unbalanced her. With the determination that had gotten her through months of therapy and later carried her through medical school, Sara jerked her mind back from that unnamed edge. She rolled onto her side. This time she tucked a small throw pillow between her knees. The pillow kept her hips aligned comfortably, so that her bad hip wouldn't stiffen up too much while she slept.

She closed her eyes. Later. She'd think about all this later. Right now she had to sleep or she wouldn't be alert tonight, when her patients needed her.

Ten minutes later she slept.

Memorial Hospital was a new building in an older part of the city. Some of the homes in the area were shaded by hundred-year-old elms. The nearest residents belonged to professional clubs, historical associations and the Junior League. They parked Volvos and Mercedes in their curving driveways, along with the occasional sports car.

Not so very far away, however, lay a section of Houston that was neither new nor old. Simply tired. Poverty wore down a neighborhood fast. For three blocks on either side of that stretch of Burroughs Avenue, people were careful about what colors they wore, who they spoke to. The gangs had moved in two years ago.

Sara lived in the pleasant section, not far from the hospital where she worked. Normally she drove her four-year-old Ford Taurus to work. That night she rode in Raz's black-as-night muscle car. He made conversation while she sat, stiff and mostly silent and all too aware of him.

Even after she arrived at work she was aware of him nearby, watching. She didn't like it. She didn't like the way her eyes kept straying toward him, or the fact that she felt safer with him there. Oh, she really didn't like that. Her independence was too dearly won for her to appreciate his presence or the way it made her feel.

Halfway into her shift, Sara stood at the nurses' station, writing out a prescription for the toddler in 3-B. Raz stood at the end of the hall, talking to one of the security guards. At least he'd hidden his gun and shoulder holster beneath a jacket tonight. Not that he would win any fashion awards. He wore a beige sports jacket with a green T-shirt, dirty running shoes and those sexy, faded-to-white jeans.

"Too dreamy for words," a young, nasal voice was saying. "What do you suppose he's *doing* here, anyway? The way he keeps staring gives me goose bumps."

Sara's eyes flickered up. She saw him standing there. Watching. It didn't matter what he wore, did it? People noticed him. Women, especially, looked at *him,* not his clothes. They thought about what lay under those clothes, and whether they could get him to turn that smile on them.

Sara knew that, because she kept having the same thoughts.

"Hadn't you heard? He's Dr. Grace's bodyguard." That came from Lynn Daniels, a cheerful dumpling of a woman. She was an excellent triage nurse, and the only person on this shift who was shorter than Sara. "Quite a hunk, isn't he?"

"Dr. Grace?" Jenny Burgoyen's round face turned toward Sara. Her eyes were big with astonishment beneath eyebrows plucked to thinly penciled lines. "He's *yours?*"

Was it so amazing that a gorgeous man would associate with her, even for pay? Sara handed the prescription to the charge nurse. "Not exactly," she said shortly. "I'm only renting, not buying. Foster, please see that 3-B's mother gets this prescription."

Jenny giggled, Foster took the prescription, and Lynn handed Sara the next patient's chart. "Is the boss back yet?" Sara asked. She hadn't forgotten her decision to talk to her supervisor again about whether she was more of a hazard than a healer while Javiero was on the loose.

"Not yet. I told her you wanted a word. Oh, the blood gases are back on 2-A."

Sara nodded. Before she realized it, her gaze had slid down the hall again.

He was there. Watching. Making her feel safe…making her heart give a stupid, excited little jump.

It took more of an effort than it should have to slide into the professional persona she'd built so carefully over the years—cool, calm Dr. Grace, the woman with nerves of steel. The woman who hardly noticed that her new bodyguard was standing in front of the same wall the security guard had smeared with his blood two weeks ago.

* * *

Raz watched Sara turn away and head for an examining room at the other end of the hall. He felt cramped, restless and altogether too close to the edge.

A cigarette would have helped. That's what he'd done before when the present made him twitchy—reached for a cigarette. But the things he'd done in the past to cope hadn't worked out very well, had they? Reason enough to quit, he'd decided two months and three days ago.

He'd been in a hospital then, too. Funny how life worked out.

His reaction to being in a hospital again came as an unpleasant surprise. He hadn't known he'd developed a phobia about hospitals until he'd followed the pretty mouse into this one. How should he have? After all, he didn't dream about the ambulance ride he'd taken two months and two days ago, or the emergency room where he'd ended up. And this wasn't even the same ER.

But it smelled the same. They all smelled the same, like blood and misery and disinfectant. The examining tables looked the same, too. He remembered. God help him, he remembered all too clearly lying on one of those damned tables, bleeding and begging someone to tell him about Marguerite.

And now here he was at another hospital, trying to keep another woman from being gunned down. Raz leaned against the wall, his hands in his pockets, his attention split between the ER entrance and the woman walking down the hall toward him. Life was sure funny, all right, he thought as Sara Grace started to pass him by without a glance. One big, damned, ugly joke. "Where are you going?"

She paused, her lips tight while her eyes avoided his. Those pretty lips of hers had been tightening up all afternoon, ever since he didn't kiss them. "What does it matter?"

"Think about it. My job—guarding you? It's a little easier if I know where you are."

"Fine, then," she snapped. "I'm on my way to the ladies' room. After that, I'll be in Examining Room 4-B, then back at the nurses' station, probably. Then I may get to go to the break room for a cup of coffee, unless my boss gets back or we get some new patients."

He chuckled. "You're a lot different once you sling that stethoscope around your neck, aren't you? Ornery. I like it."

"Did I ask what you like?" she muttered, but a hint of color touched her cheeks, and her eyes skittered away from his. "Now, if you'll excuse me—"

"I remember you now," he said, unwilling to have her move away quite yet. "Once I saw you in your doctor clothes, the night we met came back to me."

She stopped still, and looked at him.

"I'd been drinking."

"I noticed."

He shrugged. "I was Eddie at the time, and the people Eddie MacReady was hanging out with didn't understand abstinence." If he hadn't been slightly fuzzed by alcohol, he wouldn't have needed the twelve stitches she'd put in his arm. Normally he managed to avoid bar fights—or at least avoid getting cut in one.

She hesitated. "Being undercover…I guess you have to blend in."

Only if you wanted to stay alive. "One way to avoid doing the hard drugs yet stay in character is to have a reputation for being real fond of the legal ones. Like bourbon. That's Eddie's preferred poison." Raz might have blamed his failure to recognize Sara on the alcohol that had hazed his mind when he first saw her over six months ago, but he couldn't afford the smallest self-deception anymore. The fact was, he hadn't remembered her because she seemed like a different person here at work.

The change in her intrigued him even more than it bothered him, and he didn't know why he had either reaction.

A small smile touched her lips. "Do you often talk about yourself in the third person?"

"Eddie isn't me." But thinking about a night when he was being Eddie helped him block memories of another hospital on another night. He remembered Sara's hands best. She had graceful hands, the palms narrow and elegant, with long fingers ending in the short, scrubbed nails of a hairdresser or a surgeon. He remembered watching those deft fingers as they sewed him up. He'd been convinced there was something unique about her hands. Something magical.

An alcoholic fancy, of course. And yet he was surprised he hadn't recognized her hands as soon as he saw them again.

She started to speak, but he never found out what she would have said. An ambulance crew called to say they were coming in with two of the victims of a three-car collision, and she hurried away as if she'd forgotten he existed.

He'd already noticed how unmouselike she was when she wore her doctor clothes. The woman he saw in action when the first victims were brought in was even more of a revelation. For the next several hours he watched his subject, the nurses, the halls and the patients. He flirted when he got the chance, and he considered ways Javiero might try to get to his target and how to counter those attempts. And some of the time, when the memories of another emergency room rose too near the surface, he distracted himself with other questions.

Who was Sara Grace, really? And what would her hands feel like if she touched him as a man instead of a patient?

Having company on the ride home from work felt strange to Sara, and there was something alarmingly intimate about riding in Raz's low-slung muscle car. Christmas lights jeweled the darkness outside the car and reflected off the windows. Music, low and bluesy, throbbed from the speakers. It was not the sort of music she would have expected him to pick, yet somehow it fit. The car itself smelled of leather and cigarettes.

He hadn't spoken since she slid in next to him at the ambulance entrance.

The silence worked to make her more conscious of him, not less. After a few blocks she had to break it. "Do you smoke?"

"I used to."

"What made you decide to quit?"

He didn't even look at her as he signaled, then turned smoothly onto Highpoint. "Health reasons."

Her fingers drummed once on her thigh. Twice. Irritation

made it easier to speak. "Look, you did suggest we'd deal with the situation better if we got to know each other."

His voice was low and husky. "That wasn't the only thing I suggested, as I recall. Though I didn't exactly put the rest of it into words." He glanced over at her, his expression impossible to read in the shadowy interior. "I had the impression you turned me down. Was I wrong?"

Her hands clenched in her lap. He was doing this on purpose. He wanted to rattle her, she was sure of it, even if she couldn't imagine why. "As *I* recall," she managed to say in a cool little voice, "your only other suggestion was that I not go to work. I did turn that down, yes."

He chuckled. "You know, before going in to work with you tonight, I had the idea you were shy. Now I've seen you in action, and, honey, 'shy' is not the word I'd use to describe a woman who straddles a 250-pound man on a crash cart."

"The patient was epileptic. He went into convulsions."

"Yeah, and you were just doing your job, right? Nothing wrong with that. Nothing wrong with the suggestion you made to me tonight, either." He grinned.

"I didn't—I haven't—we hardly spoke."

"Oh, talking isn't necessary for this kind of suggestion. Did you think I wouldn't notice the way you kept sneaking peeks at me? If there's anything particular you want to see, honey, you let me know. I'll be glad to show you."

Mortification swept over Sara in a red tide. He'd noticed? Oh, no. Why hadn't she tried harder to control her eyes? He just looked so *good* to her. Her eyes had been drawn to him over and over, but she hadn't thought he'd caught her at it.

"Hey," he said more gently, "I'm not—*hell!*"

She had time to blink. That was it. The next second he tramped on the gas and spun the steering wheel, flinging her sideways and sending the car into a wide, crazy turn. The terrible thunder from her nightmares mingled with the explosive sound of the back window shattering. Glass pebbles rained over her head and shoulders.

Javiero! It must be. She pushed herself upright just as the car leaped the curb, but Raz's hand left the gearshift long enough to shove her head down. She stayed down, bent double over her seat belt, as the car spun through another wide turn, no doubt gouging huge tracks in someone's lawn. Then they bounced hard—once, twice—and were back on pavement.

The car shot forward, fishtailing slightly.

Sara didn't *decide* to move. There was no room for thought in the chaos crowding her brain. She raised her head because she simply had to see what was happening.

They weren't escaping. Javiero stood in the middle of the street. They were barreling down on him at sixty miles an hour and picking up speed.

Four

She caught a single glimpse of the face of the young man who wanted to kill her—a face too old, at twenty, to belong to a boy, yet far too young to look so ancient and empty. He clutched his gun tightly, his mouth hanging open as if he were screaming at the crazy man trying to run him down. Then he dived between two parked cars, and they went whizzing past.

Sara would have tried screaming herself if she'd thought of it in time. Everything happened too fast, though. Raz slammed on the brakes. The car's rear end swung wide, and their momentum spun them around. They were skidding sideways down the road when she saw the reason Raz had braked so suddenly. Her breath caught and held.

A big, dark-colored delivery truck was headed right for them.

One moment they were skidding sideways. The panel truck was close, so close. Its headlights blinded her, conjuring up an old, old nightmare. Maybe she *was* screaming—or remembering screams.

The next moment she bounced violently as they accelerated into another spin—harder, wilder, around and around they spun, like a child's toy car.

Seconds later they stopped. Dead. Smack dab in the middle of someone's front yard. A string of still-burning Christmas lights twinkled merrily on the hood of Raz's car. The headlights picked out something metal and crumpled on the front fender.

She remembered to breathe.

"I don't see him," Raz said. "Dammit, I told you to stay down." His hand enforced his opinion by pushing her head between her knees. She gulped in another breath and heard his door open.

She didn't rise up all the way. Just enough to see him throw himself out of the car and crouch with his arms extended, the deadly black metal of his gun gripped in a two-handed search. There was enough light from a nearby porch for her to see him clearly. Enough light for Javiero to see him, too. Sara watched, dizzy and breathless with fear.

It occurred to her that her breathlessness might have something to do with the way she was bent over her seat belt. She fumbled for the release, but her fingers were stiff and useless.

Raz turned in a circle, gun extended. Blood trickled down his cheek.

Other instincts kicked in. Somewhere nearby a car motor revved up. She ignored it. The seat belt parted beneath her suddenly sure fingers. Tires squealed off down the street as she scooted over and half fell out of the car.

Raz was staring off down the street. "Hell," he said, lowering the gun. Then he saw her. "Hell and damnation. Didn't I tell you to stay down? That means stay in the car, you little fool."

"He's gone. He must be gone, or you wouldn't have lowered your weapon." She wasn't dizzy anymore. No, now she wanted to laugh or scream or maybe run in circles very fast. Soon, she thought, she would have a mega-case of the shakes. Soon she would start to feel the bruises from the seat belt and shoulder strap that had kept her from more serious injuries. Right now, adrenaline was zinging through her system, making her feel like a pinball on speed. She looked around. "Where's the other driver? The one in the van?"

"Four blocks away and hauling ass. Javiero—in case you're interested—took off in a late-model Chevy."

"Good." She came toward him. "Now hold still. I want a look at that cut."

He scowled at her. "What cut?"

"The one that's bleeding." She grabbed his head and angled it to catch the glow from the porch light. She could tell the laceration wasn't deep. A couple of butterfly bandages would take care of it. "How did it happen?"

"I don't know." He frowned impatiently. "I've got to call this in."

"You aren't a cop, you're a bodyguard. Hold still." She gently probed his hairline, jaw and cheekbone with the fingers of one hand while gripping his face with the other.

"Ow!" He pulled away. "What the hell are you doing?"

"I don't think anything is broken. There could be a hairline fracture, though. You should have X rays."

"I don't need any damned X rays. Nothing is broken."

She reached up and grabbed his ears this time. "You're too high on flight-or-fight now to even know if you're hurting. Look at me. I want to see your pupils."

He scowled at her. She ignored that. Injuries, physical weakness of any sort, made some people angry. She understood that very well. His pupils were equal in size and no more dilated than they should be, given the low-light level.

And his irises were dark, lick-me chocolate.

Uh-oh. She didn't want to scream or run in circles after all, though her heart was pounding hard enough for a marathon runner approaching the finish line. No, there was something else she wanted badly to do with the witches brew of chemicals inciting her system to riot. "You seem to be all right," she said crisply.

"That's what I told you."

"Good." She still had a grip on his ears. She used them to pull his head down. Then she kissed him.

Later. Later she would try to understand what she did, and why. Now all she wanted was the feel of him, the startled look in his wide-open eyes when she pressed her lips to his. What she knew, what she didn't know, didn't matter. This did—this heat, the vivid life in him that called to her. His scent, musky and male. The way his eyelids started to droop over those candy-kiss eyes—oh, yes, that mattered.

Her hands traveled down his body because she craved his warmth, the beat of his heart beneath her palm. He was alive. Intact, unhurt. A tremor moved through her, a wave built of fear and desire. It was both familiar and foreign enough to make her pull back and look up at him, her eyes wide, her body humming.

She saw the faint flush on his cheekbones, the heavy-lidded gaze that met hers, and she blinked, amazed. She'd done that? With her kiss, her touch, she'd aroused this man? Bewildered, she stammered, "I...I don't know what I'm doing."

He smiled. "Do you not? Well, pretty Sara, I do." He framed her face in his two big hands and bent his head to hers.

He knew, all right. He knew how to use his tongue when he kissed, how to stroke and tease and persuade. Yes, she thought, dazed by the needs that rose, quick and tangled, to confuse and beguile her. Her mouth opened. She didn't know if she responded to his wishes or her own. She didn't care. He tasted like coffee and dreams, and she couldn't move. How could she move when she wanted to press closer as badly as she wanted to run away?

When he raised his head, her breathing was seriously disrupted. So was her mind. Not until then, when his mouth was no longer on hers, did she hear a voice nearby. Quite a loud voice, coming from the porch with the light on, ranting about reckless drivers.

Oh, my. They were standing there kissing each other in someone's front yard, weren't they? Someone whose Christmas lights were snagged on the hood of Raz's snazzy black car. Someone who stood on his front porch now, screaming that he'd called the police already and he had their license number, so they'd better not even think about trying to get away.

"Later," Raz said to her, smiling. "Later, sweetheart, we'll pursue this subject. Now I'd better go persuade the citizen whose Santa I mowed down that I really am one of the good guys."

One of the good guys? Not likely, Sara thought. It was a thought that had come to her, off and on, for the past few hours. Surely a good guy didn't take advantage of a vulnerable woman that way. Even if she *had* kissed him first.

"Shock," she muttered as she crept around the corner of her house, a bowl of tuna fish in her left hand. "A perfectly natural reaction to danger. That's all it was."

The sun was barely creaking up over the unseen horizon, and she was as tired as a first-year intern. Too tired to feel insecure about being outside when a murderer was stalking her. Of course, the fact that two uniformed officers were watching over her little house helped, too.

"My adrenal medulla was stimulated, after all," she told the bushes—quietly, so the officers wouldn't hear. "With all the epinephrine and norepinephrine disrupting my system, it was no wonder I..."

Except that it *was* a wonder. She didn't understand how she could have done such a thing. Good grief, she'd actually grabbed a man and kissed him. And not just any man. Her fantasy man. Who also happened to be her bodyguard...who would be back any minute now to take her away. For several days, probably. The two of them, alone together for days and days...

Sara muttered a faint, unsatisfactory "damn" and crouched to peer beneath the rhododendron. Her bruises hurt. So did her hip, but not enough for her to need to baby it, so she didn't.

Where was that blasted cat? She couldn't leave without him. Packing and leaving so suddenly was hard enough to do.

She simply wasn't an impulsive person. She certainly wasn't decisive, not outside of her job. There, she took charge because she had to. When she had a patient she forgot about herself and did whatever needed to be done. But when she wasn't practicing medicine, she was one big, quivering mass of dithering doubts.

Every other day of her life, at least, she had been. Apparently danger was a more potent aphrodisiac than she'd realized.

She sighed, impatient with herself. Then she glimpsed the big, battle-scarred tomcat she was searching for. At least, she saw two glaring yellow eyes way back in the shrubbery. They were spaced widely enough apart to belong to the ungrateful beast. "C'mon, MacReady. I know you're not afraid of me, so quit sulking. Come on out and eat." She set the dish down. "MacReady?"

"I know Raz is a little peculiar at times," a voice said behind her, "but he hardly ever needs to be coaxed out from under the bushes."

By the time she turned around, still kneeling, Sara had her breathing enough under control she could hope not to look like a scared rabbit. She couldn't do a thing about the blush heating her cheeks. "Lieutenant Rasmussin," she said to the tall man standing a few feet away. "I, uh—I wasn't calling your brother."

"I'm relieved to hear it, ma'am." A smile tilted one corner of his mouth.

"It's my cat," she said quickly. "Well, he's sort of mine. He doesn't really believe that yet, but I've been feeding him, so I can't go off and leave him now. But I don't think he'll take well to traveling, or to a cat carrier, so I've put a sedative in his tuna, one the vet recommended. But he won't come out and eat. Do you think he knows something is up?"

Tom studied the woman kneeling by the big bush. She looked ready to fall over, and he suspected the babbling was a symptom of exhaustion as much as nerves or embarrassment. "I think he knows you want him to eat it, ma'am, and he's ornery enough—and suspicious enough—for that to make him hold back."

She glanced at the bush and sighed. "Maybe if I leave it here, he'll think he's stealing it. I suppose that would appeal to him more."

"I imagine it would." The cat wasn't that different from some people Tom knew. One in particular, who was worrying him considerably at the moment. "Where is my peculiar brother, anyway?"

"The cat carrier," she said, and pushed stiffly to her feet. Tom thought her hip must be bothering her. "He went to get that and a couple of other things. He took my car," she added, looking guilty. "His is getting fixed. It…there was some damage last night. From the bullets."

Raz went after a *cat carrier?* Instead of hustling his witness to safety? "I told him I wanted you out of the city as soon as possible."

"And I told him I wasn't leaving without my cat."

Tom looked at her standing there, pale and puffy-eyed from lack of sleep, bruised and frightened and, he suspected, about as hard to deter as the average avalanche once her mind was made up. He smiled. Maybe things would work out yet.

The sound of a car door told him his brother was back.

"Do you know where this safe house is that he's taking me?" she asked.

His smile faded. *Not bright, Raz. This is not a woman who will appreciate being kept in the dark.* "He didn't tell you?"

"I think he's mad about his car getting banged up. All he does is smirk or growl. I don't really care where we go, except that I need to be able to swim."

Tom heard footsteps and turned his head. Raz was walking toward them. He wore his usual ratty jeans, this time with scuffed boots and a plain white cotton T-shirt. He held a pet carrier in one hand. "You can swim where we're going," he said. "If you don't mind cold water."

Tom glanced at Sara Grace again. She wore jeans, too. Hers were nearly new, neatly pressed and topped by a short-sleeved sweater with big, yarn-covered buttons. It was pink, a soft, pretty pink that matched the flush in her cheeks when she met Raz's eyes. "So where are we going? Near the ocean?"

"Very good, doctor." Raz gave a mocking little bow. "Now, where's this great big kitty you didn't want to crowd into an ordinary-sized cat carrier?"

"Under there." She gestured at the bush behind her.

"You're kidding."

Her chin came up. "He's shy."

The scowl Raz turned on her should have sent a timid woman like her scuttling for cover. It didn't. There was enough heat in the way Raz was looking at her to steam puddles right off the sidewalk. And she was looking back.

Tom couldn't decide if he was looking at disaster about to boil over—or his brother's salvation. He shook his head. "Why don't we step up on the porch, Dr. Grace, and see if that gives your cat enough room to make him feel safe?"

"Oh." It was obvious from the startled way she blinked that she'd forgotten he was there. "Oh, yes, of course. Would you care for some coffee, Lieutenant? I'm leaving the pot here, so it would only take a minute."

"Damn straight you're leaving the pot here," Raz muttered. He set the carrier down and started for the porch. "And we don't have time for you to—what in the world is that?"

He was looking at the large cardboard box that sat on the porch next to a suitcase.

"I told you I'd be ready to go when you came back," she answered evenly. "This is what I'm taking with me."

Raz stepped onto the porch and glanced in the box. "The medical journals I can understand. But the cooking stuff?" He shook his head. "Believe it or not, I'm not taking you so far away from civilization that you won't be able to buy flour."

She joined him on the porch. Tom was a step behind, but he doubted either of them noticed. "I doubt very much I'd be able to find fresh rye flour or whole-wheat bread flour in a nearby grocery store, no matter where we end up. Certainly nothing of this quality. I special order my baking supplies."

Raz glanced at the box with every evidence of loathing. "And the yarn?"

"My knitting. I have to have something to *do*," she said, spreading her hands. "We'll probably be gone for days. I have to do something with my hands."

Raz smirked.

Tom spoke before his fool brother could say whatever stupid thing was on his mind. "Looks like you're going to get some homemade bread, Raz. If you don't make the doctor too angry to feed you." He faced her. "Ma'am, I did come by for a reason."

"Yes?"

"We haven't been able to learn how Javiero discovered your identity, but I think we have to assume that his information came from someone at the hospital."

"Oh, no, I'm sure you're wrong. No one at Memorial would put me in danger that way. What possible reason could they have?"

"Fear. Greed. Guilt. Many of the things people do are based on one of those motives, Dr. Grace. I know it's difficult for you to believe, but everything indicates that someone at the hospital did tip off Javiero. Until we have some way of narrowing down the possibilities, I have to ask that you have no contact with anyone here, except through me. I'll be in touch every day."

After a moment she nodded, pale but steady. "All right."

"If you have others, friends or family members who live out of town, that you need to contact so they won't worry—"

She was shaking her head. "I've taken care of that. I left a message on my answering machine saying that my aunt broke her ankle and I was flying up there to take care of her for a few days."

Raz frowned. "Your family is bound to know that your aunt didn't break her ankle."

"I have no family except for my aunt, and she won't call. I left the message in case one of my friends from back home—

from back in Connecticut—should try to contact me. I assume I can call my machine occasionally and check for messages?''

Raz looked like he wanted to argue with her. Tom answered before his brother could put his foot in his mouth again. ''That shouldn't be a problem. By the way,'' he said, nodding at the shrubbery behind her, ''I think your cat is about finished eating.''

''What?'' She turned to look at the bushes, where a huge marmalade tom was licking the bowl she'd set down. As if the animal sensed their attention, he paused to glare at them warily. ''Oh, thank heavens.'' She smiled. For the first time Tom caught a glimpse of what she looked like when she was happy. *Why, she's really pretty,* he thought, surprised.

Then he saw the expression on his brother's face as Raz watched her, and his anxiety tightened another couple of notches. Disaster or salvation? Whichever she might turn out to be for his brother, he was beginning to worry about what Raz intended to be to her.

Sara was still smiling, looking relieved and pretty and very tired. ''I was worried that he might refuse it, but he's eaten every bite. I checked with a vet on the dosage. The acepromazine should knock him out pretty quickly, and we can leave.''

''That's not a cat,'' Raz said, staring. ''It's an orange bear cub. Or a mutant.''

''Mac—'' She broke off before she finished naming the animal. Color flared in her cheeks. ''Mac has had a hard life.''

''Maybe so, but it sure didn't stunt his growth. Unless he really is a bear.''

''If you want to go see if you can get him in the carrier, ma'am,'' Tom interjected, ''I need to brief your bodyguard here on a couple things.''

''That animal is too big for her to handle,'' Raz said. He started for the steps.

She put out a hand to stop him, irritated. ''I may limp, but I'm not a weakling. I'll take care of it.''

Raz hesitated. Tom could see the clash in him, and he understood it. He and Raz had been raised by the same man, after all. Their father firmly believed that there was man's work and there was woman's work, and the harder, sweatier and nastier the job, the more certainly it fell into the man's column. Over the years, Tom and Raz had worked with enough female officers to loosen the grip of that early training. But it hadn't disappeared.

Neither had Tom's need to take care of his little brother, even if that meant kicking his butt. Maybe especially then. "I need to talk to you," Tom told him.

Raz's lips tightened. He gave a nod. Sara Grace moved down the two steps off the porch. She was limping, all right, but Tom didn't doubt she could take care of that big beast she said was hers. He wasn't as sure she could handle the other beast that was prowling around her. The one Tom was related to.

"So," Raz said, facing his brother. "What weren't you telling her? Is there a definite tie to the hospital?"

Apparently Raz's hormones hadn't completely taken over his brain. "The local vice boys and girls have been investigating some brand-name pills that have turned up in the Padres' turf in the past few months. They figure the pills had to have come from one of the area hospitals, and circumstantial evidence points to Memorial as the source."

Raz's lips tightened. "What kind of quantities?"

"Nothing major. It looks like someone has been grabbing whatever they could get their hands on easily."

Raz nodded. Tom knew he didn't have to explain how that might affect Sara. If someone at the hospital had been selling narcotics to the Padre leader, Javiero could be blackmailing him or her now for information on the witnesses. Sara Grace needed to be cut off from everyone at the hospital.

"I'll make sure that investigation gets stepped up. And now," Tom said, his voice low, "you're going to tell me what the hell is going on with you and the woman you're supposed to be guarding."

Raz lifted one eyebrow. "You know, I could have sworn I did that already. Which part did I forget to mention? The way

Javiero tried to take Sara out last night? Or that we're heading for the beach house today?''

"I am in no mood for your smart mouth, little brother. What are you thinking of, getting involved with a subject you're supposed to be guarding?''

"We're not involved," he said. But his eyes followed the woman they were talking about, who was following a retreating orange tail around the corner of the house.

"Don't give me that. I'm starting to feel like a voyeur, watching you watch her. You remind me of a stallion when he gets the scent of a mare in heat in his nostrils.''

Raz's fists clenched. The anger Tom had seen simmering in him the past two months looked ready to boil over. "If you're saying Sara is—''

"I'm saying I can't afford to have my witness jeopardized by an idiot who's thinking with his balls instead of his brain. You go ahead and get her out of town, but I'm going to send someone from North's agency down to relieve you as soon as I can get it arranged.''

"Look," Raz said, "you manipulated me into doing this. It was supposed to be for my own good, right? My own good. Lord, that's a joke. You set me to guarding a woman because you thought that would be good for me. Particularly if I can keep this one from getting killed, right?'' His mouth twisted. "Well, now you can stay out of it. Officially you don't have the authority to interfere in Dr. Grace's private security arrangements. Unofficially you can get your nose out of my business.''

"She's my witness. That makes her my business.''

"Don't worry about that part of it. You were right about one thing. I'll do whatever it takes to keep her alive.''

Something in Raz's voice chilled Tom. "Stop sniffing around her. She's not up to your weight.''

"I tell you what—why don't you let me worry about how well she takes my weight? Like she said, she's no weakling.''

Tom grabbed Raz's arm. "I am not going to let you use that woman to soothe yourself with.''

"To *soothe* myself? You think I find it relaxing to walk around stiff with something other than pride? Get real." He jerked his arm out of Tom's grip. "I'm not looking for her to soothe me, but you can quit sweating about your witness's virtue. I won't seduce her. Just play with her a little."

Tom shook his head. "I don't know what's going on with you. Do you think you can play with a woman like that without hurting her? Do you think you can play with the kind of sexual explosion that's brewing between the two of you—and stop?"

"Yeah, that's exactly what I think. You don't know as much as you think you do, big brother. I'll stop, all right."

"You've got a helluva lot of confidence in your ability to—"

"You don't get it, do you? It's not my *ability* that makes me so confident. Just the opposite. You know I crossed the line two months ago, don't you? It's on my record. That's supposed to be confidential, but you wouldn't have any trouble getting a look at it, would you? I know you, Tom. You got hold of that record right after I said I was quitting the force."

He didn't deny it.

"So you know what happened on my last assignment. I slept with a source. With the girlfriend of the scum I was trying to put away. But what you wouldn't know, the part that didn't get into the report, was that Marguerite thought she was in love with me."

"Raz," Tom said, helpless. "What happened that night wasn't your fault."

A muscle jerked by Raz's mouth. "Of course not. Her mistake, right? She took two hollow-point slugs for making it. By comparison, I got off pretty light. All I had to deal with was a single bullet, a little time in surgery. That, and this other little problem I have. With impotence." He turned, jumped off the porch and walked away.

Raz ignored both his brother and his client while he loaded her car.

Ignoring his brother worked pretty well. Tom left without speaking to Raz again, thank God. Raz knew only too well you could never stuff the genie back in the bottle, or unsay words once they'd been spoken. That didn't keep him from regretting the anger that had led him to humiliate himself. With any luck, he wouldn't have to face his brother again for a good, long time—long enough for them both to pretend he'd never said a word about impotence.

Ignoring Sara didn't work as well.

He loaded the box of cooking and knitting supplies in the back seat, then carried both their suitcases to the trunk. The mouse didn't drive what he thought of as a "doctor car." Her modest little four-door sedan was dark blue, in good condition and handled like a crate.

Raz had her trunk open and was glaring down at its contents when he heard her approaching.

"I got him." She staggered around the corner of the house, holding the cat carrier in front of her with both hands. And she wobbled, dammit. Oversize animal plus oversize carrier equaled too much weight for one small, slightly damaged woman, and he didn't care how blasted independent she wanted to be. He stalked over to her and grabbed the carrier out of her hands, turned and walked back to the car.

"Well." She dusted her hands on her jeans. "Thank you. I guess."

A low, ominous rumbling sounded inside the cat carrier as he stowed it in the back seat. "I thought you tranquilized him."

"I did." She followed him to the car, where she hefted one of the suitcases up onto the back bumper.

"He doesn't sound tranquil. You probably forgot to mention that he's a giant mutant when you asked about the dosage." And that was *his* suitcase she was balancing on the car's bumper while she frowned into the trunk. He closed the door and leaned against the back bumper, one eyebrow raised. "You're having trouble finding room for that, maybe? Since you've got a Christmas tree in your trunk?"

"It's a very small tree."

He shook his head. "Baking supplies. Knitting. And the Christmas tree from your living room. Look, sugar, you can't take your whole life with you when you're hiding out."

"I'm not going to miss Christmas." Balancing the suitcase on the bumper with one hand, she bent and reached into the trunk, obviously trying to shift things around. "It's a big trunk. There's room."

He should help her, but, damn! He didn't want that Christmas tree in her trunk. He didn't want it trailing along with them like the gaudy ghost of everything he'd lost. "Christmas is still twelve days away. There's every chance you'll be home in time."

Her words were punctuated by grunts as she shoved at something in the trunk. "Christmas isn't—only one day. And this isn't—exactly—home." Apparently she got things settled to her satisfaction, because she returned both hands to his suitcase. She lifted and heaved. He felt the car rock slightly beneath the weight of his suitcase as it landed in the trunk.

When she looked at him, her eyes were soft with sympathy. "Though I do hope we're back in time for you to spend Christmas with your family."

Raz felt as low-down as a snake on a reducing diet. Maybe right this moment he didn't plan on ever setting eyes on his brother again, but he knew he'd get over that. The fool woman looking at him with such sympathy didn't have anyone to avoid or to seek out. She didn't care where she spent Christmas because she had no one to spend it with. Just that damned tree and her mutant cat.

So why didn't she hate the holiday as much as he did?

He looked in the trunk. She'd gotten his suitcase in on top of the box of ornaments, but the tree still took up most of the room. It sat there in a huge plastic bag, lights and garlands still strung, leering up at him. He sighed. "There's no room for your suitcase in here." He grabbed it and headed for the driver's side, where he opened the rear door.

The cat was growling again. Or still. "Get in the car," he

told Sara, and then he said a few more things under his breath as he shifted things around in the back seat. By moving the driver's seat up far enough to give him leg cramps, he got the suitcase in. Barely.

Sara still hadn't gotten in, however. "What are you waiting for?" he snapped. "We've got nearly five hours of driving ahead of us, and I'd like to get on the road."

Her hands opened and closed nervously. "It's my car."

"What?"

"It's my car," she said a little louder. "I'd prefer to drive."

"Oh, yeah. Right. You aren't trained in evasive tactics. You haven't had any sleep in—"

"How much sleep have you had?"

"That's different. I'm used to it."

Now when she met his eyes there was a spark of anger in hers. "Don't patronize me. I've worked back-to-back twelve-hour shifts in the ER. There may be any number of things you can do better than me, but staying alert when you're short on sleep isn't one of them."

"And what happens if Javiero is trailing us? Will you know what to do? Will you even know what to look for?"

She rubbed her hip with one hand. "Your brother has had men making regular sweeps of the neighborhood. Javiero won't see us leaving, so he won't follow us."

"My brother is not infallible, or he would have already caught the little bastard." He sighed. "Look, it's not likely that I'll need to do anything but stay awake and fight the traffic on the way out of town. But you're paying me to keep you safe. Let me do my job."

Her chin tilted up. The hand that wasn't rubbing her hip clenched in a fist. "Like you did last night, you mean?"

"You have some complaints about the way I saved your life?"

She looked away. Raz might have taken the two spots of color high on her cheeks for anger if the rest of her face hadn't been so pale. "Never mind," she muttered. "I prefer to drive myself, that's all. It's not important.'' She rubbed her hip absently as she turned away.

Her hip. Her pallor. Suddenly he understood. "How did you hurt your hip?" She stopped to look at him, her narrow eyebrows drawn together in a frown over those tired, winter blue eyes. He persisted. "Was it an auto accident?"

She stared. "You're good, you know that?" She looked away, one hand still rubbing at what would never be completely healed. "It happened a long time ago. A very long time. And usually it doesn't bother me, but last night reminded me.... I don't remember the accident itself, but I remember our car going over the divider. And the headlights. They were coming straight at us. I remember the headlights."

Raz made his decision instantly. "Here," he said. "Catch."

She caught the keys reflexively and looked from them to him, her brow wrinkled.

"Do you know how to get to Highway 59?" he asked, moving around to the passenger's side.

"I—yes, I think so."

"Good. Head south on it to Victoria, where you'll need to switch to 77. Wake me before we get to the intersection with 181," he added, sliding into the car. He reached for the cellular phone she kept in her car. "I'll need to give you more directions then." He punched in a number he knew better than his own and in a few moments he'd arranged for an unmarked police car to escort them out of the city.

She slid in behind the wheel. "Thank you," she said quietly.

"Hey, I'm not a jerk all the time. I do know how to compromise." He tried a grin.

She met his eyes. It was a mistake, he wanted to tell her— because as soon as he looked in those big, pretty eyes, he remembered. He remembered the awkward way she'd grabbed him and kissed him, and her shocked surprise when he kissed her back. And the shy way she'd opened her mouth to him, the eager way her hands had clutched at him.

He forgot to control his expression, and what she saw there made her blush and look away.

Her hand trembled slightly as she put the key in. "Thank you, anyway," she said, "for finding a compromise. I'm not very good at that."

"No problem." He found the lever that let him recline his seat, used it, and closed his eyes.

Raz was too aware of the woman beside him to fall asleep, but he knew how to fake it. That was his problem. He was too damned good at fakery. But some things couldn't be faked. Like integrity…and the ability to make love to a woman.

It was just as well, he thought as the car accelerated to highway speed, that he couldn't have the pretty mouse. The tattered remnants of his own honor wouldn't have stopped him from having her in his bed tonight. Or maybe having her on the couch this afternoon. Even if he couldn't make love, there were plenty of things he could do to her, things that would let him look and touch…

No. No, he wasn't going to torment himself and hurt her that way. He hadn't needed his brother to tell him Sara wasn't the kind of woman a man should play sexual games with. No matter how much fun those games promised to be.

He would keep his hands off the pretty mouse, he told himself. And with that somehow comforting promise, he fell asleep.

Five

The change in speed woke Raz. He straightened and looked around.

The day was sunny in spite of the halfhearted drizzle dampening the pavement. He recognized the small town they were entering. He'd been through it often enough, both on his own and when he was a kid.

He smiled. His mother had dragged him and Tom to several of Victoria's historic homes when they were little. He'd gotten in trouble for climbing on the old steam locomotive in Memorial Square, and he'd eaten a picnic lunch at the park bordering the Guadalupe River. He took a moment to enjoy the memories conjured by the small town of Victoria as Sara pulled into a convenience store parking lot.

"Anything wrong?" he asked.

"I'm wiped out," she admitted, braking to a stop. "You'd better take over."

He stretched, scratched his stomach, rubbed his face and

came fully awake. "Okay." He reached for the door handle. "I think I'll get some coffee. Want anything?"

"That's it?" she said. "That's all you're going to say, after the fuss I made about driving?"

"One of my better traits," he said cheerfully, "is that I never say 'I told you so.' Besides, if I hadn't thought you had the sense to wake me if you needed to, I wouldn't have given you the keys."

The sun was shining right through the drizzle. He ambled toward the little convenience store, enjoying the stretch and flex of cramped muscles, the dampness on his face, even the bite of hunger in his belly. For some reason, today felt like a good day to be alive. The edgy anger that had enveloped him earlier seemed to have evaporated while he slept.

He couldn't see any reason for his new mood, but it had been a long time since the hum of anticipation had quickened his blood like this, putting an edge on life that sharpened his senses. He wasn't about to question it.

When he got back to the car, Sara was in the passenger seat. Sound asleep.

She didn't wake when they pulled back out into traffic. No surprise. Her face was pale with exhaustion, the skin under her eyes smudged with shadows. All in all she looked as frail and breakable as one of those porcelain figurines his mother collected.

Appearances sure could be deceiving.

They reached Aransas Pass at noon. Raz had his window down. He wanted the smell of the ocean in his nostrils, that vast and lusty mingling of salt and fish and decay. High overhead, dirty gray clouds skidded along at a good clip, covering the sun. Out over the ocean, more clouds piled up dark promises of storm. Raz figured he had time to get a few groceries and still reach the beach house before the rain hit. Maybe.

Sara didn't stir when he pulled up to a small grocery store. He smiled. It looked like the mouse slept with as much determination as she did everything else. When he came back to the car she stirred slightly, but didn't fully wake. He shook his head as he started the motor. She even slept neatly. No snoring, not a single little ladylike grunt when she shifted position. Her dark hair was still tidy, too. Of course, it was short, and so fine it reminded him of fur—soft, silky, warm. He wanted to pet it.

Damn. He forced his attention back to driving.

An island-to-island causeway led from the mainland town of Aransas Pass six miles out into the ocean, almost, but not quite, reaching Mustang Island. Raz was a mile out on the causeway when he realized he was whistling.

He was almost…happy.

It was probably temporary. Nothing had been solved or resolved. But for the moment he felt good. He didn't even crave a cigarette. He whistled the refrain from "Gilligan's Island," which seemed appropriate, given the weather. Then he switched to the Irish jig his father had whistled on long car trips to this very place. Maybe, he thought, it was coming here that had wrought the temporary healing. Maybe he'd needed to return to a place enlivened by childhood memories. Or maybe…

He glanced at Sara. She was finally stirring, blinking her eyes and frowning as if she hadn't decided whether she was really awake or not. Maybe, he thought, it was the decision he'd made about her. Maybe that was the reason he felt better than he had in a long time.

"Where are we?" she said, looking around. There was little to see except water and sky. "Uh…I know you said you were taking me to the ocean, but I kind of pictured some land being involved."

He chuckled. "We're about four miles from Mustang Island. The town we're headed for is called Port Aransas. It's right on the northernmost tip of the island." Yes, he felt good about his decision. He hadn't needed his brother to tell him he needed to keep his hands to himself.

"So there is dry land at the end of this road?"

"Sure. We take a ferry for the last thousand yards or so, when we cross the Corpus Christi ship channel." That limited access was one very good reason to bring her here. "You'll like Mustang Island. The entire Gulf side of the island is beach, and the fishing—do you like to fish?"

Her tongue came out to lick her lips. "I don't know. I've never tried it."

"I'll teach you," he said. Yes, teaching Saint Sara how to fish was a good idea, much better than teaching her how to…he cleared his throat. "There are a couple things I need to tell you. You'll need to know our cover story."

"A cover story? Why would anyone care who we are?"

"That's the other thing I need to tell you. The place I'm taking you to isn't a safe house owned by the city."

She shrugged. "The city, the state, the feds—I don't imagine it matters."

"It's owned by my parents, actually."

Silence. He glanced at her, trying to gauge her reaction. She stared straight ahead, giving him few clues. "Some of the people here know me," he said. "My family has been coming here for vacations, either together or separately, for better than twenty years. So you and I will need a cover story, some excuse for us to be here this close to Christmas."

She was still silent. Not a good sign, he knew. But he'd always felt that confessions, like nasty medicine, were best undertaken all at once. He pulled something out of his pocket. "Here, put this on."

She stared at the small gold ring he held out, as motionless as if he were offering her a snake.

"It will work best if we pretend to be newlyweds."

"No! No, that's not a good idea. I'm not good at—at pretense. I won't be able to fool anyone."

"Listen, you don't have to worry." He was glad he could reassure her honestly. "I'm not going to take advantage of the situation. We may have to hold hands and look at each other all mushy-eyed sometimes in public, but leave that part to me." He grinned. "I can lust in my heart with the best of 'em. But trust me. That's where it will stay."

"Oh," she said in a small voice, and, reluctantly, took the ring.

"I'll keep my hands to myself," he said, slowing as they neared the end of the causeway and the ferry that would take them to the island. "I promise."

Damn the man and his stupid promises. Sara put her nightgown next to her undies in the top bureau drawer. MacReady, freed from his carrier, sat by the closed bedroom door. His twitching tail made her think his feelings mirrored hers.

"Don't like being cooped up, do you, Mac?" she said sympathetically as she took a small stack of shirts out of her suitcase.

She had to stand to one side to open the next drawer because there was so little space between the bed and the dresser. The Rasmussins' beach house was comfortable rather than fancy. It had a long, inviting front porch that was several feet off the sandy ground because of the uneven lot. The two bedrooms were small, but the living area was big enough for dancing. Raz was out there now, putting the groceries away in the kitchen corner of the big room while she unpacked her things.

She'd been shocked when she learned he'd brought her to his family's vacation home. And she didn't believe all those terribly reasonable reasons he'd given her. Oh, there was a certain logic to it. The place was clean, free and available, and Javiero surely couldn't find her here. The gang leader had shown himself surprisingly resourceful about tracking down witnesses so far, but there was nothing to link her to this place.

Nothing but Raz, her noble protector. The idiot.

Did he really believe the only reason he'd brought her here was because Javiero wasn't likely to find them? They could have gone to dozens of other places if that were the only reason. No, for some reason *he'd* needed to come here. Maybe it had something to do with this leave he was on.

She knew so little about him. Sara wanted to find out more, a lot more. And not just because of the way he kissed…well, okay, that was a large part of it. No one had ever kissed her like that before. As if he truly wanted her. As if she mattered.

She supposed glumly that their kiss had revealed a few things to him, too. Like her lack of skill. It wasn't as if she'd *never* been kissed before. She just hadn't had a lot of practice. Particularly not in the past two years.

All right, she admitted, pacing two steps over to the tiny closet. It was more like three years since she'd had a man in her life. And that was if she included Roger in the rankings. She wasn't at all sure Roger counted. He *was* a man, though. And she had kissed him. Twice. Once at the end of each of their dates. Still, her one and only encounter with real intimacy—with sex, she corrected herself, determined to be honest—had been even longer ago. Back in med school.

She heard the front door open and close. He must have gone back to the car for another load.

Had Raz promised to keep his hands to himself because her kiss had bored him? She winced. If so, she wasn't sure she wanted to change his mind. But what if he thought he was being honorable?

"Well, Mac," she said as she picked up her overnight case, which held her toiletries. "You have any suggestions? How does a woman go about letting a man know that the lack of sin in her life is more due to a lack of opportunity and courage on her part than to any great virtue?"

Mac watched her out of slitted eyes without replying.

"You wouldn't be any help, anyway," she muttered, carrying her overnight case around to the other side of the bed, where a closed door led to the bathroom shared by both bedrooms. "All a female cat has to do is twitch her tail a few times and smell right to get your attention. It's a little more complicated for me."

Sara opened the bathroom door and sighed. She'd never shared a bathroom with a man before. Sharing such a personal space struck her as uncomfortably intimate. And just how, she asked herself, was a woman who thought that sharing a toothbrush holder was the height of intimacy supposed to let a man know she would like him to seduce her?

Raz could do it, she thought as she set out her shampoo and conditioner. After the way he'd kissed her, making her forget everything except the feel of him, the taste of him, the long, slow slide into heat and need, she knew he could help her get beyond the shyness that kept her from attempting intimacy.

But why would he want to?

A knock sounded on her bedroom door.

"I'm back here," she called out, frowning at herself in the mirror. Since when did she give up on a project before she'd even started? Probably all she really needed to do was get him to notice that she was willing. She might not know much about men from firsthand experience, but she'd heard other women talking. From what she could tell, men were almost always interested in sex. As long as it didn't compete with football.

"Sara?" Raz called through the closed door.

He was used to seducing women, after all. That was clear. Once she got his attention, surely he'd take it from there.

"Back here," she called out a little louder. But her next words got jumbled up with his, as they both spoke at the same time. "Watch out for the—"

"Where do you want the—ouch!" The increase in volume indicated that her door was open. "Dammit, you mutant monster, come back here!"

"Oh, no!" She ran out of the bathroom and through the bedroom, pushing past Raz into the everything room.

The front door stood open, and MacReady was nowhere in sight.

Raz tried. He looked for the damned cat for an hour, right along with her. The sad look on her face would have kept him looking much longer, but the storm hit then. There wasn't much point in looking for the animal in the middle of a downpour.

"Mac will be fine," Sara assured him now from the corner of the room that served as the kitchen. He'd thought she might want a long nap after they ate their late lunch. Instead she'd started making bread. She was wrist-deep in dough now, and the rich scent of yeast filled the house.

She'd noticed the radio, unfortunately. It was tuned to a station playing Christmas music.

"Of course he will," Raz agreed. It was raining buckets out there. Any sensible animal would certainly be holed up someplace warm and dry. Were mutants sensible? He reached for another colored ball. Decorating the little tree was his self-assigned penance for losing her cat. "That creature knows how to take care of himself. Besides, rain might melt witches, but I've never heard of it affecting demons."

"Is your hand hurting?"

She'd insisted on taking a look at the scratches her demon cat had left on his hand in the process of making his getaway. "It's fine." It stung like blazes.

"At least he didn't bite you." She moved over to the sink, where she washed her hands.

"Oh, yeah. That's good. Did you get your bread all kneaded or whatever it was you were doing?"

"It has to rise now." She turned, drying her hands with a paper towel. His attention was drawn to those hands. Such long, clever fingers, graceful and efficient...with a simple gold band on the third finger of her left hand.

She was wearing the ring, just like he'd told her to. It meant nothing. There was no reason for this odd twisting feeling in his gut.

"I didn't mean that a bite would hurt any less than those scratches," she went on, amused. "But puncture wounds are harder to disinfect properly and can do a lot of damage to a fine, crowded piece of engineering like a hand."

"Crowded engineering?" His mouth twitched in spite of his sour mood. "Is that how they taught you to talk in medical school?"

Her cheeks flushed. "Oh, in medical school I would have said something about the crowded metacarpal region, with the ulnar and radial arteries, the synovial membrane, the dorsal, palmar and interosseous ligaments, the—''

''I get the idea,'' he said dryly. She looked so very domestic and pretty standing there, all flushed with pleasure at their mild banter. He went back to studying the tree. ''Almost finished here.''

''It looks nice.'' She drifted closer. ''I really think Mac is okay, don't you?''

''Definitely.'' The song on the radio switched from ''Silver Bells'' to ''Jingle Bell Rock.'' He felt as jittery as a water bug. If he stood still too long, the surface tension would break and he'd sink.

Sink? Into what? He put his hands in his pockets and tried not to think.

''I know it was a lot of trouble, bringing the tree here,'' she said apologetically. ''I probably should have just bought another one. But I spent so much time picking this one out. It isn't easy to find a small tree with such a nice shape.''

Some small things came in very nice shapes indeed. He was careful not to look at her. ''I guess not.'' He pulled his hands out of his pockets and moved restlessly over to the old-fashioned stereo cabinet his father had brought out here nearly twenty years ago. It didn't play tapes or CDs, but the radio worked at least half the time.

Raz knelt and started fiddling with the knob. ''Jingle Bell Rock'' faded out, replaced by static. Even static sounded better to him than Christmas music, but he kept fiddling, trying to find another station. ''You really get into Christmas, don't you?''

''Oh, yes.'' She picked up one of the few remaining ornaments without commenting on his changing stations. It was a delicate glass angel with frosted tips on her wings. ''It's the rebel in me.''

His eyebrows went up. ''You see celebrating the holiday as a rebellion?''

''My aunt didn't want to, you see. It wasn't a religious preference. She just doesn't like fuss.'' She hung the little

angel near one of the lights and tipped her head, studying the
effect. Then she moved one of the fake icicles he'd hung. "My
mother loved Christmas, though, and I made a promise to myself that I'd always celebrate the season, come hell, high water
or Aunt Julia." She glanced at him with one of those confiding
smiles. "I can be pretty stubborn at times."

"No kidding." He finally got the radio to admit there were
other stations. Alan Jackson started singing that everything he
loved was killing him. Raz grimaced and stood.

She glanced at him. "You like country music?"

Anything was better than another round of Christmas carols.
"It's okay. So you hung on to your Christmas traditions in
spite of your aunt. That must have been difficult." He moved
uneasily over to the windows that made up most of the south-
ern wall. Rain lashed the glass, obscuring what was usually a
pretty decent view of the ocean.

"It wasn't easy. I was sixteen when my mother and my
father were killed and I went to live with my father's sister.
Aunt Julia is—well, she's not a happy person. Solitude suits
her. Now that I've moved out, she's pretty much of a recluse."

"She took you in, but she didn't give you a home." The
nastiness outside soothed him slightly. He stood with his legs
spread, staring out at weather that resembled his insides.

Surely that blasted cat had found a place to ride out the
storm.

"That's right. You're very good, aren't you?" She moved
a shiny red ball a few inches, making room for a tiny elf
holding an even tinier package.

He shrugged. "A cop who doesn't learn how to pick up the
clues people leave about themselves gets stuck in traffic patrol.
I hated traffic patrol."

"You're good at that, too, but I meant that you were good
at getting people to open up."

"Yeah. People trust me," he said, not bothering to hide the
bitterness. He walked along the length of the window wall,
restless again. Was the wind slowing, the rain maybe not
drumming quite so hard?

"What did you do on rainy days when you stayed here as a kid?"

He frowned at her, puzzled by the sudden jump in topics.

"You're obviously not very good at rainy days." She smiled, then bent over to dig around in the ornament box. The view was attractive enough to stop his pacing for a moment. "You look like Mac does if he's cooped up inside for more than five minutes. I tried to make him a house cat when he first came around," she added, straightening. "It didn't work."

"Your cat will be back," he said automatically.

"Oh, yes. Except—" She looked down. One last angel dangled from her hand, a frivolous bit of cloth and yarn with her glittery halo slightly askew. Sara's shoulders drooped. "He doesn't really know he's my cat, you see. And this is a new place. He may not feel obliged to return."

"Hey, obligation doesn't come into the picture with cats. That beast of yours is no dummy. You've been feeding him for a while, right? He's going to remember that. He'll show up again when he gets tired of making it alone out there."

She looked past him, out the window. The weather chose that moment to make a point. Lightning tore a hole in the curtain of rain, loosing a vicious blast of thunder that made the muscles along Raz's shoulders tighten reflexively.

Sara flinched.

The movement was slight, but he couldn't stand it. She was supposed to have that cat. He started for her. "Listen, the storm seems to be letting up a bit."

She turned incredulous eyes on him. "You think so?"

"Sure. I'll be able to go out soon and look some more." He stopped a pace away, looking down into her serious eyes. His hand lifted without his conscious decision. He stroked her cheek, finding such silk and softness as he'd forgotten existed in this world. "I'll find him," he promised, knowing he might not.

"You're a good man," she said softly.

Now *he* was the one to flinch. His hand dropped. "We should probably divide up the kitchen duties."

She smiled. "You can't mean cooking. I saw what you bought—canned chili, canned spaghetti, canned soup. That's not cooking. You obviously have no taste buds."

Oh, yes he did. Only they were fixated on one taste. Her taste. "Hey, I'm very discriminating. Health conscious, too. I'll show you at supper. A little of that Tabasco sauce in the turkey chili—"

"Raz." She stepped closer.

Uh-oh. "You feeling okay?" he asked weakly.

"I'm fine." She wasn't looking at his face. Slowly, deliberately, she placed her left hand in the center of his chest, fingers spread, palm flat. The gesture conveyed a peculiar blend of innocence, curiosity and possession. His ring, that fake ring, winked up at him from the third finger of that claiming hand. "Why do you ask?"

She was curious. About him. His heartbeat kicked into high gear, while his voice dropped, involuntarily, to a lower pitch. "You look rather...flushed."

"Do I?" An inch at a time her gaze crept up while her hand stayed where it was. It was only one small hand, he told himself...one small hand with a wonderfully warm palm and long, clever fingers. A hand he'd been trying hard not to fantasize about.

"I had the impression," she said breathlessly as her eyes finished their journey and met his, "that you think I'm—that you—well, you seemed to like kissing me." She immediately flushed scarlet.

He knew what to say, what to do. He'd let her down gently. "I did." He put his hand over hers to remove it. He was going to move it and tell her why he couldn't take her up on her offer. "I liked it very much. Only—" Only somehow his lips were very near hers now, a whisper away. A breath— "You definitely should not do this," he told her. Or maybe himself.

Just for a moment. He would allow himself only a moment

to kiss pretty Sara who looked so sweet, but tasted of spices and storms.

Her lips were soft beneath his, soft and giving. Then she surprised him. She took his lower lip between her teeth. It was such a small, shy nip, so timidly erotic.

Raz had no defense against innocence. Lust ripped through him, as quick and hot as if he'd never before held a girl or taken a woman. He made a noise low in his throat when he pulled her against him. He had the crazy notion that if he could just hold her close enough, long enough, she could warm the cold place inside him, the winter place he dreamed of where blood spilled so red against the white, white snow. But he couldn't hold on to her, could he? He had to stop.

He *would* stop. Just as soon as he got her to open those pretty lips to him again. "That's perfect, sweetheart," he whispered against her parted lips. "Perfect." His tongue teased its way inside, but he'd stop soon. Very soon. He had to. He'd promised…

Her other hand joined the first one on his chest. They were curious, those hands. They made inquiries of his chest and then his stomach. One of them ventured all the way down to his waist, then teased up under his shirt just enough for her fingertips to ask shy questions of his bare skin.

He shuddered because he knew the answer to those hesitant questions. Yet he'd promised…what? What had he promised? Something about his hands?

Yes. His hands. She wanted his hands on her. She told him that with the shy explorations of her own hands. But his hands weren't shy, no, they knew where to go and what to do. At the moment one of them was cupping the back of her head, holding it at just the right angle for his kiss. He used the other hand to begin unfastening the big buttons on that soft pink sweater.

"You want me to touch you, sweetheart?" he murmured against her neck, finding a hollow where her scent gathered, light and wildly intoxicating. "Oh, yes, you do, don't you?

You'll like this," he told her, as he slipped his hand over her not-quite-bare breast.

She felt good, so good, but he was supposed to stop. He did remember that, dimly. For some reason he was supposed to stop. And he would, he would—but her body pressed against him eagerly, and the low, happy sound she made in her throat as he rubbed her breast told him she didn't want that any more than he did.

What he wanted, needed, was more of her. He wanted her on her back. He needed more of her bare so he could look and touch, nibble and taste.

Ah. The couch was right behind them. Wonderful.

Sara's head was spinning. No—the whole room was spinning as Raz's strong arms lifted her, then laid her down on something that felt cozy and giving against her back. He followed her down, lying alongside her, one of his legs between hers, his thigh heavy and warm right where she needed it. Whether by accident or instinct, he kept his weight from her bad hip, and his mouth was eager on her throat as he unfastened her bra.

Then he touched her bare breast. She gasped. His palm was hot. His fingers were firm and sure, teasing her nipple, pinching and rubbing and making her body lift from the couch, an instinctive supplicant. And he knew, oh, clever man, he knew. His head lowered. He licked her nipple, circled it with his tongue, laved it and incited it. Then he sucked. Sara's world splintered into shiny pleasure fragments that sorted and reformed themselves with every breath in an erotic kaleidoscope.

When he lifted his head she had no idea why he'd stopped—indeed, she had no ideas at all, only needs, bright and dark blended together in a swirl of sensation. Certainly his damp lips and the heated blindness of his eyes told her nothing about stopping.

Then she heard it. Knocking. At the door.

He rolled off her. The sudden loss of him, the cool air on skin that was normally warm and dry and *covered*, shocked her into thought. She lay on the couch in an untidy sprawl, both breasts naked, one wet from his mouth, her sweater and bra unfastened and—oh, my. Even her jeans were undone, she discovered as she sat up. The top button, anyway. He'd done that and she hadn't even noticed.

He was very good, she thought as her shaky fingers hurried to put the pieces of clothing back where they belonged. Very…skillful. And wasn't that what she wanted? What she needed?

Raz moved swiftly to the door, and Sara forgot the question. His face startled it out of her. Because there was no expression there, none at all.

Six

Raz didn't expect trouble. There was very little chance that Javiero stood on the porch. Even if he had somehow found Sara, the only way onto the island was by boat, and the only public access was the ferry run by the Texas Department of Transportation. The TDT people were keeping an eye out for anyone matching Javiero's description.

But Raz assumed nothing. The life he'd lived for the past eight years had taught him that much. He peered through the peephole his father had put in years ago and saw a dingy gray sky. But the rain had slowed to a drizzle while he was on the couch, occupied and oblivious, so he had a clear view of the person standing on the porch.

After one tense moment, he sighed.

This was definitely one of those good-news, bad-news situations. He glanced over his shoulder. At least Sara had her clothes back together, though the soft, rumpled look of her made it obvious what they'd been doing.

Obvious, at least, to this particular visitor. He swung the

door open. "Olivia," he said, resigned but not quite able to summon a smile.

The woman standing there was an inch below his own height. Her frizzy blond hair was at least an inch shorter than his. Her shoulders and biceps were as beautifully developed as her chest, and looked much more youthful than her leathery, smiling face.

"I don't care how mad you are. You still have to call me Livvy, you ass," she said cheerfully. "Harry's going to kill me if this isn't your cat."

Raz cravenly insisted on making the coffee while the two women got acquainted. He wasn't up to dealing with Livvy's sharp-eyed curiosity, and he didn't feel a twinge of conscience over abandoning Sara. This was Livvy, after all.

Olivia Holland was a law unto herself. She was also their neighbor on the island. She was loud and pushy and she talked too much, generally displaying all the tact of a three-year-old. No one knew just how old she was. She had at least ten years on Raz, probably twenty, maybe more. Once, about five years ago, she'd propositioned him. But that was before she found Harry.

Raz had always been a bit sorry he'd turned her down. Livvy could be enough to try the patience of a saint at times, but she had a heart even bigger than her mouth...not to mention a body that a much younger woman might envy.

The age difference hadn't stopped him. The fact that she was a friend of his parents, and perfectly capable of mentioning intimate details at awkward moments, had.

Livvy exclaimed at length over Raz's sudden marriage. She'd heard the news from Mary over at the gas station. The gas station was only place on the island Raz had stopped, but, small towns being what they were, it hadn't taken much to get their story circulating. Livvy had thought she was going to die of curiosity before she could come up with an excuse that

Harry would accept for her coming over. Wasn't it lucky Sara's cat took a liking to her?

"I've never seen him accept anyone the way he has you," Sara said.

"I've got a warm lap and I know where he wants to be petted." She chuckled. "That's all it takes to make any male purr, honey."

Raz had fiddled with the coffee as long as he could. He turned, carrying three steaming mugs on a battered Coca-Cola tray. "Don't let Livvy fool you. She's an animal magnet. Creatures of all sorts turn up on her porch."

Sara and Livvy sat on the couch together, looking about as opposite as two women could. Livvy made him think of driftwood, tough and sturdy and unique. She wore a striped tank top and turquoise sweatpants that were currently accumulating orange hair from the purring turncoat in her lap. Sara—well, she looked like Sara, small and quiet, her hair as dark and fine as Livvy's was blond and frizzed, her eyes big and wistful as she watched Livvy petting her cat.

"I'm glad Mac picked your porch to get out of the storm. I was a little worried about him," Sara admitted softly.

"Here." All of a sudden Livvy shifted Mac from her lap to Sara's. Cat and woman looked equally startled. "Stupid cat's getting hair all over me. No, you stay there, big fellow." She rubbed Mac along the side of his face the way she'd been doing. "All cats like to have their heads petted, but they each have their special spots. This one likes to be rubbed firmly right along his jawbone. See? You try it."

Raz brought the coffee over and sat down, unnoticed, while Livvy gave Sara cat-petting lessons.

"He's purring!" Sara said, delighted.

"Sure he is." Livvy sat back, looking pleased with herself. "Never had a cat before?"

"My mother was allergic to them. We had a parrot, Mr. Cleaver, but my aunt didn't...I wasn't able to keep it. Anyway, I've been feeding Mac for a while, but I haven't really managed to make friends.''

"Looks like you're doing just fine to me." Livvy's eyes drifted up to meet Raz's gaze. "Looks like you did pretty well for yourself, too! A doctor, by God. She sure isn't the sort I'd pictured you ending up with. Pretty as can be, though, and unless I miss my guess, tougher than she looks. More like a dandelion than one of those silly hothouse orchids I've seen you out with."

He lifted one brow. "You're comparing my new bride to a weed?"

Sara blushed and looked so guilty at the lie that he could only hope Livvy didn't glance her way. Livvy snorted. "There's not much prettier than a few bright yellow dandelions scattered around a lawn. Only idiots with an obsession for Bermuda grass call wildflowers weeds."

"Livvy doesn't approve of lawns," Raz explained. "Or regular gardens. She claims it's because she's into naturalization, water conservation and native plants, but in fact, she's just lazy."

"I've got my priorities straight. Speaking of which…" She eyed Sara speculatively. "You could use some tone in those deltoids. You're not flabby, mind. I can see some strength there, but no definition. I could show you a few things to do about that."

Sara looked confused.

"Livvy is the local health maven," Raz said. "She has a gym, and plenty of opinions she doesn't hesitate to share. I'd planned to introduce you—later," he said, giving Livvy a reproachful glance. "We'll see about getting you a temporary membership so you can use the pool there. I did promise you'd be able to swim."

Livvy smiled, delighted as always to find someone who paid the proper attention to fitness. No doubt she thought it only right that a new bride had made her groom promise she'd have access to workout facilities on their honeymoon. "Swimmer's muscles. I should have known. You probably don't want to bulk up, then.'' She shook her head. ''I have the hardest time persuading swimmers to add a few simple resistance exercises to their routine. Bicep curls, though. You could give them a try.''

''I'm not really interested in, uh, bulking up.'' Sara was fighting a smile. ''I swim because of my hip.''

Livvy looked curious. ''What's the matter with it?''

''The joint was badly dislocated in an automobile accident many years ago.''

''Sciatic nerve damage?''

''Yes,'' Sara said, her eyebrows lifting in surprise. ''I was fortunate there was no permanent paralysis, because reduction was delayed due to an incorrect diagnosis.''

They fell to discussing range of motion, joint stability and muscle groups. He wasn't surprised by Livvy's knowledge—the woman had been a physical therapist among other things in the past—or at how quickly Sara relaxed with her. After all, this was Livvy. Raz was content to let them carry the conversation.

He stared out the big picture window and thought about snow and cold. A few minutes ago he'd been plenty warm, while seducing a surprisingly willing mouse on the couch.

Damn, damn, damn. A man who couldn't keep a promise wasn't much of a man. Yet he'd felt like one. He'd been hard and hot and ready, and if Livvy hadn't shown up when she did—

''Raz? What do you think?'' That was Sara's voice, sounding uncertain. He dragged his attention back to the women on the couch and mentally replayed the last part of the conversation. Something about a party—uh-oh. ''I don't think we'll be able to make it, Livvy.''

Livvy laughed. ''Now, you two have to come up for air sometime. It's settled. I'll expect you at my place this Wednesday. Bring Harry a present. Doesn't matter what it is, long as it's wrapped. He's just like a kid at Christmas.'' She stood, beaming at them. "And now I'll let you get back to what you were doing when I showed up. About time, huh, Raz?" She laughed heartily. "You can quit sulking now. I'm going."

Sara turned a fiery red. Raz sighed. "Come on, Livvy. I'll show you to the door."

As soon as the door had closed behind their uninvited guest, Sara spoke. "I like her." Her body was curved gracefully into the couch as she twisted to face him. From this angle he could see that she had the beginnings of a love bite on her throat. He wanted, badly, to put his mouth there and finish the job.

He ran a hand over the top of his head. "Everyone likes Livvy. That doesn't keep people from wishing her to perdition now and then."

"I didn't know how to turn her down about the party. All those people thinking we're married..." She sighed unhappily. "This pretense must be awkward for you. Surely we could tell Livvy the truth."

He was still *hard*, dammit. This was one hell of a time for his condition to decide to cure itself—or whatever the hell was happening to him. "Oh, yeah, great idea. The way Livvy keeps her mouth closed, by noon tomorrow there wouldn't be more than fifty people who would know exactly why you're here."

She flushed and looked away. "Look, I just don't like it, that's all. And surely the lies must be hard on you. They're your friends."

"Come on, honey. You know better than that. I told you, didn't I? I'm a very good liar." If he didn't get out of there soon he was going to grab her, and this time.... He headed for the sliding glass doors that opened onto the back patio. "I'm going for a run on the beach."

"We—I think we should talk. About, well..."

"It was a kiss," he said coldly, "with a little touchy-feely thrown in. That's all. Let's skip the postgame analysis. Stay in the house, don't open the door to anyone while I'm gone, and stay away from the windows. And see if you can figure out how to keep your hands off me from now on, will you?''

Having finished making an ass of himself, he left before the anger churning inside him could make him say anything more he would regret.

Three days later Sara stood in the kitchen holding the receiver of the phone, listening to the messages on her answering machine back home in Houston. A nurse she worked with had called yesterday, as had a librarian concerned about an overdue book. The package from her aunt hadn't arrived yet. She knew that because she'd asked her landlord to pick up her mail, and to leave a message on her answering machine if any of it looked important. A package would surely qualify as important.

Sara stood in the kitchen and frowned out the window. Raz was down on the beach, heading back from the run he took every morning. She watched his figure approach as she hung up the phone.

Who in the world was the man she'd nearly made love to?

She couldn't seem to let go of that question. There seemed entirely too many men wrapped up in one ridiculously sexy package. She'd fantasized about the good-looking bum who showed up in her emergency room one night. She'd met the cop, been teased by the seducer, warned by the liar and watched over by the bodyguard...and she'd kissed the passionate, needy man who lived inside all the others.

At least, she thought she had. But that man, if he existed, had disappeared the moment Livvy interrupted them, and he hadn't shown up again. Nor had the surly stranger who'd told her to keep her hands to herself. She supposed she should be glad of that.

She wasn't.

Every day he went for a run in the morning. Every day he told her to stay in the house, to not answer the door or the phone. So far she'd done just what he told her. She thought about that and decided it was time to stop.

Sara was accustomed to making her mind up quickly. So, once she decided on a course of action, she went straight to the back door, pausing long enough to grab her cane on the way out before starting on the path to the beach. She wasn't alone, though her companion was several yards away, had four legs and preferred to pretend he was unaware of her existence.

Livvy had suggested Sara shouldn't try to keep a cat used to roaming free cooped up. She thought it would only make Mac more frantic to escape and less likely to return when, inevitably, he did get out again. Sara had to agree, but it gave her a pang every time she watched Mac disappear out the door. Still, so far it had worked. The cat came to her more readily than before. He didn't want her to hold him, but he liked to be petted. He purred for her.

He wove his way through the grasses near the path to the beach now, giving the impression of one whose direction just happened to coincide with hers for the moment. She smiled.

The wind was sharp off the ocean, chilly enough to make her glad of the sweats she'd bought the day before. She used her cane to help her down the slope to the beach. Between the shifting sand and the workout Livvy had put her through yesterday, her calf was tingling this morning, a sure sign the muscles were stressed and undependable. The damp weather made her hip ache, too.

But not as badly as her curiosity did.

Gulls wheeled overhead as she worked her way down to the hard-packed sand left by the receding tide. Sara watched her footing and considered her poor taste in preferring the bad-tempered Raz to the charming tour guide he'd turned into. But his temper, she suspected, was genuine, while his charm was as democratic as the rain. It fell equally on everyone.

In the past three days, she'd seen the Mustang Island State Park and the University of Texas Marine Science Institute. They'd gone on a five-hour boat tour of the Aransas National

Wildlife Refuge, where she'd actually seen a mated pair of whooping cranes. Yesterday they'd gone back across the channel on the ferry so she could see the shrimpers and look at the Seamen's Memorial Tower, then gone on to the Crab-N, a restaurant that was part of a housing development built on canals. Unfortunately she was allergic to shellfish, so the Crab-N hadn't been a big success. She'd had a hamburger.

Raz didn't avoid her. He talked to her. She now knew when the island had first been settled, the name of the last big hurricane to blow through and what had been involved in setting up the Texas State Birding Facility.

She didn't know why he'd seemed to want her so much, or what had changed his mind.

Another woman might have managed to slide free of the pleasant conversational coils Raz wrapped around her with such slippery charm. Another woman might have confronted him directly over his determination to ignore anything personal between them. Sara didn't know how to do those things. Which was why, after he left for the solitary run he took every day before assuming his self-imposed duties as her vacation planner, she had decided to break one of his stupid rules and follow him.

The day was winter pale, all but colorless. Above her the sky arched in a bleached canopy that, back in Connecticut, would have meant snow. The sand beneath her feet was the neutral beige of the tile floor in the ER, as colorless as the plants that sprouted near the edge of the beach—the grasses and weeds pale and salt-silvered, like the spray Sara tasted when she licked her lips. Even the ocean that mumbled to itself beside her lacked color. But it was dark and vivid, calm on the surface at the moment, vast and unpredictable beneath.

Like the man watching her. Raz had turned to face her as soon as she started down the beach, and he waited for her now a hundred feet away. Not moving. Probably angry.

Sara was shy, but she cared about those around her. Because she paid attention, she often understood more about others than they would have guessed. So she was pretty sure Raz was fleeing some kind of demons. Something had happened to make him take leave from the police force. Something that worried his big brother, the lieutenant with the cold eyes. Something, maybe, that had made Raz run hot-and-cold toward her.

Or maybe his change of heart had everything to do with her, not him. Maybe she'd done everything wrong. When she'd been in his arms, Sara hadn't felt self-conscious. She'd forgotten doubts in the rush of sensation. Once before, Sara had known a feeling so powerful it had sliced her mind from her body, but that sensation had been pain.

It was different when pleasure took over.

Slowly she drew near enough to see Raz clearly. His black sweater made her think of spies or Irish fishermen. The wind had run its fingers through his hair as thoroughly as any lover, leaving it tousled and beautiful, while his eyes—his eyes were as brown and cold as the broken pieces of a sea-wrecked ship.

She stopped in front of him.

"What the hell are you doing here?" he said.

"I need to ask you something. It's safe enough. You've already heard from your brother this morning." Raz checked in with Tom every morning and reported the results—or lack of results—in the police's efforts to locate the gang leader.

A muscle jumped in his jaw. "You think that because Tom hasn't found Javiero yet, it's safe for you to wander around by yourself out in the open?"

"I think that Javiero is still in Houston, and that makes it perfectly safe for me to walk on the beach here."

"Assumptions kill people every day. Don't ignore what I tell you again. Good God," he burst out, "even if you have so little regard for your safety and my judgment, I'd think you would have more self-respect than to come running after me once I made it clear I don't want you along."

"I've done half of what you wanted," she said, her head high. "I've managed to keep my hands off you."

"But you haven't quit asking me to change my mind about that, have you? You followed me down here—"

"Not for *that.*" Her face went hot.

"Maybe not, but your eyes follow me all the time, and they sure as hell seem to be asking for *that.* What do you want from me? A quick tumble? I've told you as clearly as I know how, that's all you can have. And somehow I don't think you're the type who likes to sample men and then move on."

She took a deep breath. "I want you to teach me how to fish, like you said you would."

He stared at her a moment longer—then burst out laughing.

She was relieved to learn that fishing didn't necessarily involve handling worms.

"I can't believe a woman who can tuck a man's guts back inside his stomach cavity is squeamish about sticking a worm on a hook," Raz said.

He'd brought her to a jetty that jutted out from the Gulf side of the island to deflect currents from the ship channel. It was supposed to be a great place to fish, but the weather seemed to have kept everyone away except a crowd of noisy seagulls and a couple of old women in blue jeans and kerchiefs. The sky was still overcast, and the wind chopped the bay into stiff little peaks. The weather wasn't cold, not to a New Englander, but it was chilly enough to feel almost seasonal.

"Worms are slimy, like cold spaghetti," she said. "I'm sure any sensible fish will prefer the wiggly plastic things you bought." The place where they'd purchased their fishing licenses sold a great deal of tackle, too. Sara had been as amazed by all the artificial ways there were to entice a fish as she was relieved by the absence of worms.

"Worms are slimier than guts?" he asked, grinning.

"Human intestines are more slippery than slimy, actually. Not clammy like spaghetti, and not cold at all if—"

"Remind me never to get in a gross-out contest with you."

He stopped. "This looks like as good a spot as any. Let's get set up."

There wasn't much to set up. In addition to their rods and tackle, which he'd carried, she had a small tote that held a couple of soft drinks, a pillow for her to sit on if her hip got cranky and a cellular phone.

That phone was a grim reminder that this wasn't really a holiday. Raz kept it with him all the time so his brother would be able to reach him if anything broke in the case. There had been other reminders of her status in the past three days, such as the way Raz insisted on being the first to enter the cottage when they returned to it. Sara considered his caution excessive, but she didn't argue.

"What kind of fish did you say we're after?" Sara set her pillow near the edge but didn't sit. She was excited about learning to fish.

Among other things. She gave her teacher a quick, nervous smile.

"Anything that will bite." The smile he gave back to her was as natural as it was intoxicating, and it had as much in common with the pleasant charm he'd hidden behind the past three days as the sun had in common with a candle. That easy smile did a better job of warming her against the brisk wind than her jacket.

Raz had dug the beige windbreaker out of a closet and told her to put it on. Like the rod and reel she would use today, it belonged to his brother. They'd had to roll the sleeves of the jacket up practically double to let her retain the use of her hands. Between that and the billed cap he'd stuck on her head just before they left, she supposed she looked silly.

She didn't care, not once he finally gave her a real smile again.

"We'll try for some redfish," he went on, handing her his brother's fishing rod. "They like this depth at this time of year. Or we might get a speckled trout. Uh—you aren't allergic to all kinds of fish, are you?"

She shook her head, smiling. She felt like laughing for no particular reason, except that it was so nice to have *this* Raz back. "Only shellfish."

"We can hope to catch our supper, then, since I can guarantee you won't get shrimp or lobster like this. You're ready to go," he said, nodding at her rod. "I've put a quarter-ounce jighead on with the plastic bait. That should give you enough heft in this breeze. Give it a try."

She looked from him to her rod uncertainly. A few inches of line hung from the tip of the rod, with the soft plastic "bait" dangling at the end along with the hook. "How do I make the line go out long enough to reach the water?"

"You've never handled a rod and reel? Not at all?"

She shrugged. "My father was a lawyer, not a fisherman."

"Lawyers fish, too. Some of them. Here," he said, and moved close to her. Close enough to grip the rod near her hand. Close enough that she felt his heat all up and down that side of her. "Push on this gizmo and it releases the brake on the line. See? When you have enough line, you stop it like this."

"Oh!" She wasn't as startled by the action of the reel as she was by the way her skin tingled when his hand brushed hers. "I can see how you get it back up. You just wind this thing."

"That's right. You do that, get your line reeled back in, and I'll show you how to cast."

Casting sounded like fun—especially if he had to stand really close to her again to show her how to do that.

He did. And it *was* fun. Unfortunately she caught on rather quickly.

"That's it," he said, standing behind and to her side but no longer touching her. "Not too much line. Lift your tip as soon as the bait touches down—good. Now start reeling. Keep it moving kind of quick." He moved away and picked up his own rod. "If you slow down the retrieve too much, the lure will sink into the grass."

"That's bad?" She turned the little handle steadily.

"If you've got a fish watching that little wiggler, it will lose interest if the bait drops out of sight. You could get a bunch of grass tangled on the line, too, hiding your bait."

So she needed to keep her bait in sight, did she? Sara glanced down at the oversize jacket that hid every bit of her and sighed.

A moment later his line spun out, the jig plunking into the ocean not far from hers. Sara cast and reeled, quick and steady like he'd said. She watched him do the same, then she cast and reeled again. She listened to the waves shushing themselves against the jetty. A gull cried out overhead.

"Nothing is happening," she said.

He laughed.

She gave him an irritated look. "Well, I rather thought there was more to it than this. People make such a fuss about fishing. How long does it usually take?"

Instead of answering, he sat on the edge of the jetty. "You aren't used to being still, are you? It's funny. You seem so quiet and restful, but you are the busiest restful person I've ever seen. In fact, I have yet to see you actually rest."

"Why, I sit and rest quite often," she said, surprised.

"You sit, yes. Sometimes you read one of those medical journals of yours. For about fifteen minutes. Sometimes you drag out that shapeless mass of knitting you brought—for about fifteen minutes. Then you're up and doing again."

"I'm a speed reader," she said defensively.

"A speed knitter, too?" he asked, amused.

It was true that she hadn't made much progress with the shawl she was knitting, but she had very little free time, after all. And... "I was in traction for over ten weeks after the accident. I like to be busy now."

He reacted with no more than a flicker of sympathy, a casually interested glance that was infinitely easier to bear than pity or distress. "How old were you when you were hurt?"

"Sixteen."

"It's hard to be still at that age."

She didn't answer right away. Silences usually made her uncomfortable, as if there was something she should say or do to bridge the gap in the conversation, something she was too socially inept to grasp. Somehow, this pause felt as natural as the ebb and flow of the waves.

One of the seagulls swooped low over the water, looking for fish or garbage. Another one landed on one of the pilings about ten feet away. It cocked its head to study her with one dark, beady eye. Sara nodded at it as she reeled in, watching the taut arc of her line. "See that fellow watching us? He won't sit there long. He's fidgeting already. Birds aren't still unless they're sleeping. And the fish we're hoping to catch— they don't stop moving unless they're dead. I'm not comfortable with doing nothing."

"I'm not good at sitting still myself," he said. The tip of his rod sailed back, then forward as he cast again.

She glanced at him dubiously. He looked pretty relaxed.

"Really," he said, grinning. "That's one reason I like this kind of fishing. I can't pace in a boat."

"You like to pace while you're fishing?"

He shrugged. "Here I can set down my pole and move around if I get the urge. I don't like being confined. Stakeouts are one of my least favorite parts of police work, because you're tied to one spot. It's better than working a desk job, though. And as for bed rest—well, the last time I was in the hospital—" he broke off.

She glanced at him, curious at his sudden silence. "I didn't think I was that hard on you when I stitched up your arm."

"Not that time," he said. "Not when you stitched me up. A couple months later…I'm a lousy patient," he said, and shrugged. "My nurses probably bribed the doctor to release me early. What about you? Were you a good patient, or a little hellion?"

"I did everything they told me to," she said. "Everything. I had to. I wanted to walk again."

He paused. "You couldn't walk at all?"

"Not at first. I needed an operation before I knew…but I was determined. The doctor who treated me in the ER told my aunt to be prepared for the worst, you see. I overheard him. He thought—well, I'll spare you the technical terms. He made a quick, sloppy diagnosis and I heard it."

"You proved him wrong."

"Yes." The fierce pride she felt in her accomplishment throbbed in her, as real and sustaining as her pulse. "My aunt may not be a warm person, but she has her virtues. When I told her I wanted another doctor, she listened to my reasons. And agreed. And once Aunt Julia sets her mind to do something, she does it right. She found me some of the best people in the field."

"But you don't give your doctors all the credit, do you? You know who did the work."

"I couldn't have done it without them, though. Having the right doctor on your side, one who does the right thing at the right time, makes so much difference. Especially…"

"Especially in the emergency room." He reeled in, pausing before he cast out again. "That's why you went into trauma medicine, isn't it? Because you wanted to make sure people weren't given a hasty diagnosis or the wrong advice at such a crucial time."

She shrugged, self-conscious. "It sounds arrogant put that way, but—yes. I'm good at what I do." She glanced at him. "What about you? What made you choose police work? Was it because of your brother?"

"Tom? No, he would have been a good reason for me to become an accountant. He's a hell of an act to follow." His reel whirred as he cast.

She hesitated. "You two seem close."

"We are. That doesn't mean he doesn't drive me crazy. You don't have any brothers or sisters?"

"No."

"Cousins?"

"No. No one like that. My aunt never married, and my mother was an only child." She reeled in steadily, looking at his stony profile instead of the water. "You don't want to talk about yourself at all, do you? You ask me all sorts of—"

All at once something struck her line and pulled. Unprepared, she wobbled and nearly fell in. "Raz!"

"You've got a fish! Hey, that's—watch out!" He dropped his own rig and hurried to her.

She probably could have steadied herself. She probably could have brought the fish in on her own—eventually. But it didn't hurt to have Raz's arms go around her, locking her to him. It didn't hurt to lean against him while he helped her with the rod and reel that seemed suddenly alive, fighting to jump out of her hands.

The fish broke water in a quick, silver flash.

She leaned her head against his shoulder and laughed. "This is fun!"

He looked down and his eyes were laughing, too. At first. Laughing and open, as free as the boy he'd once been. But they changed. From one pulse to the next, his eyes lost their innocence.

Sex. Raw and basic, that's what she saw, a hungry, growling need that made her shiver in alarm and arousal. She saw sex in his eyes.

And she saw herself, reflected off the shiny mirrors of his dark irises.

That quickly, Sara lost something. It passed from her to him as surely as if she'd handed it to him. Her heart beat harder, faster, as if it were racing after that lost bit of herself. Her lips parted because she needed suddenly to taste the air around him. She needed to breathe him in, to hold some part of him inside her the way he'd just taken something of her into him.

Something? *What?* she asked herself, panic brushing her with the first, frantic beat of its wings. She had no answers, no words—but he saw, he knew. On some level, at least, he knew what was happening to her. She could see that knowledge hit him in the flare of his nostrils, in the deepening awareness in his eyes.

He lowered his head, as if he were about to kiss her.

Confused, she moved her head in the tiniest negative.

His arms fell away. He stepped back, and his gaze was as opaque now as it had been open a second ago. "See if you can land him yourself," he said so politely she wanted to weep. "It's better if you do it. You'll enjoy it more that way."

No, she thought. Her head bent as she tried to focus on the rod and reel that had started bucking in her hands again as soon as he took his strong grip away. No, she'd done everything herself for years and years now. She knew all about independence and solitude, knew she could continue to live that way if she had to. But she didn't think doing things alone was better. And she was quite sure she wouldn't enjoy it more that way.

Seven

Clouds were shredding themselves on the sickle moon when Raz and Sara walked to the party that night. Wind tugged at the gaily colored gift sack in his hand and whipped Sara's long skirt against her legs. Her cane was a subtle silver flash in the darkness. The only light came from the streetlight a block behind them, and from the multicolored twinkle of Christmas lights on some of the houses they passed.

"Mac didn't much like being left inside, did he?" she commented.

Raz grunted something that the woman limping beside him might take for agreement if she wanted.

She was silent a moment before trying again. "I think Livvy will like the ornament I found. It looks like one of her dumbbells. What did you get Harry?"

"Something for his collection." He didn't want to talk to Sara. He wanted to shake her. She was hurting. He knew she was, because she'd used her cane all day. But when he'd told her they would drive the block to Livvy's house, she'd set her chin stubbornly and said he could do what he liked, but she was walking.

If he'd had the slightest reason to doubt that Javiero was still in Houston, he would have insisted they drive to the party. But Javiero had been sighted in his old neighborhood only that morning, and Tom was cautiously optimistic about their chances of picking him up soon. Even if the punk didn't slip up and get caught, there was a good chance that the investigation into the stolen drugs at Memorial would result in another way of tracking him down, through the man he'd been blackmailing.

Raz hadn't told Sara any of this, of course. She was a civilian. Never again would he make the mistake of taking a civilian into his confidence in an ongoing investigation.

"Livvy said to just get Harry a present, but that didn't seem right," Sara persisted. "I felt sure we should have something for both of them."

"She always says that."

"Do you think she means it?"

"No."

That was, apparently, curt enough finally to discourage her.

To their right, beyond the thin row of houses draped in their brave seasonal finery of red and green lights, beyond the moon-silvered grasses and the pale slice of beach, the ocean called. Raz listened to that vast, murmurous female voice as it took part in the endless discussion water held with air and land. Tonight air and ocean sang an unquiet duet, while the land was silent.

Like his conscience.

He'd nearly kissed her again. Five hours later he was still in a fine fever over that almost kiss, afire with need and reckless denial. But if guilt was an ingredient in the stormy blend that stirred him, it was a silent addition. The only voices he heard spoke of her hands—such pale, clever hands. He thought of her breasts, round and perfect as the arc hinted at by the crescent moon, and he remembered the crinkly dark berries at their tips.

"Dammit," she muttered. "This is ridiculous."

He had to agree. For an impotent man to pant after a woman this way was damned ridiculous. And yet…he was beginning to think he'd lied to his brother. He didn't feel incapacitated around Sara. No, at the moment he was almost certain he could pull her down on the soft sand beside the road, push her skirt and panties out of the way and push himself inside her.

And he wasn't at all sure the damn fool woman would stop him, or that his battered sense of honor was enough to keep him from finding out whether she would or not.

But fear…fear was still a sufficient deterrent. What if his apparent recovery was misleading? What if he failed her, and himself?

And then there was his promise. "What's ridiculous?" he asked, ready to be distracted.

"This jacket. I know Livvy said the party is casual, but I look like an idiot." She shoved at the sleeves of the windbreaker that threatened to swallow her.

"When did you talk to Livvy?" *Keep talking, Sara. Don't leave me alone with my thoughts.*

She slid him one of those wary, considering looks she'd been favoring him with ever since he didn't kiss her. "I called her to ask her what to wear, when you went jogging the second time. Speaking of that—how long ago were you in hospital?"

He scowled. "What?"

She shrugged, the movement all but lost in the depths of that jacket. "You mentioned being in the hospital not long ago. I wondered if you weren't pushing your recovery a bit hard, running twice a day. What were you there for?"

He was almost too surprised at her probing to be angry. Almost. He stared hard at her profile, at the way she'd hunched her shoulders against the wind, and couldn't figure out what she was up to. "For my sins."

"Did you undergo surgery?"

"I *lived*." That was it, really—that was what cursed him to be where he was. He'd lived, when others hadn't. "But a saint like you wouldn't understand that living can be a punishment for your sins, would you? For you, living means helping others. Doing good works. Baking bread, for God's sake.''

Her chin tucked down protectively, but her voice was firm enough. "I'm not a saint. I'm a coward."

"A coward!" His laugh was bitter. "You don't know the meaning of the word, honey, or you wouldn't keep trying to get me to kiss you again. You're not real smart, maybe, but you're not a coward."

"I haven't been—"

"Are you a virgin?"

She stopped and stared.

"You kiss like one." He was thinking of her innocence, of the shyness that appealed to him too much. He hadn't said it to be cruel.

Had he?

Her face was a pale, shocked oval in the darkness. Without speaking, she started limping forward again. They went the rest of the way in silence.

Raz had taken several steps down the long, curving drive to Livvy and Harry's place before he realized Sara wasn't with him. He turned. "What is it now?"

She was staring at Livvy's home, as horrified as if he'd been leading her to Dracula's Transylvanian castle. "This can't be where the party is. Livvy said she lived at the end of the block."

"This is the end of the block." And the cars lining the driveway were a pretty good clue as to where the party was being held.

"The redbrick house we just passed was the last home on the block where your parents' house is," she pointed out with annoying precision. "This house has an entire block of its own."

"Nonetheless, this is where Livvy and Harry live." He glanced at their destination. Livvy's home was a one-story sprawl of stone and glass set in an acre of naturalized plantings. "I guess I should have mentioned that Livvy is well off."

"Rich. The word is *rich*."

Raz shrugged. "You tend to forget she has money after you're around her awhile. But, yes—she owns quite a few fitness centers, not just the one here. And some real estate. Harry handles the gyms now. That's how they met, actually— she hired him to run one of her gyms. A week later they got married. Come on," he said impatiently, "she's still Livvy, regardless of what sort of house she lives in."

Sara shook her head. "I can't go to a party at a house like that dressed like this. You go on."

Raz stopped arguing and really looked at Sara. Her feet were planted stubbornly, but that was pure terror he saw in her eyes. "Sara," he said gently. "It will be okay."

"I hate parties." There was a wobble in her voice that he was sure she hated even more. "I'm not good at them. This one will be crammed with people I don't know, all of them knowing each other and wearing cocktail dresses and—and look at me! Look at this jacket, and this s-stupid skirt."

He wanted to put his arm around her. And then he wanted to take her back to the cottage and show her how little her clothes mattered by removing them, one by one. He managed to keep from moving. "If you can't take my word for it, ask yourself if Livvy would have let you come in the wrong clothes."

"She said it was casual. People who live in houses like that think casual means to leave the sequins at home. *You* dressed up," she said accusingly. "You should have warned me."

"I'm wearing jeans," he protested.

"And a sports jacket. And a very nice knit shirt. You look very California like that. I just look—dull."

He shook his head. The sports jacket was to hide his shoulder harness. She wouldn't appreciate him reminding her of that, though. She'd already protested him wearing the gun to the party. "It will be okay," he promised again. "Livvy's parties aren't like anyone else's. Come on." And he gave in to his own needs and held his hand out to her.

Slowly she stepped forward and put a hand in his. "You'll stay with me, won't you?"

"Sure." But the trusting warmth of her hand was undoing him even as he spoke. Something inside Raz crumbled, some shelter he desperately needed. He rubbed his chest, where the cold was lodged.

Sara was infatuated with him. He knew it, and part of him wanted to feed on that, to hold her close enough that the warmth of her approval might reach all the way inside him. But it would be wrong. No, what he was going to have to do was prove to the pretty mouse how little he deserved whatever fledgling feelings she nourished for him.

He thought, with a sick sense of certainty, that he knew just how to do that.

Raz was right. Livvy's party wasn't like any other. And he did stay with her...for the first hour.

For that hour he played the devoted husband so well she had to keep reminding herself this was all pretense. He introduced her to people and stayed by her side, giving her the confidence to relax. For the first time in her life Sara was actually enjoying herself at a party.

Then he abandoned her. Oh, it was neatly done. He waited until they were talking to a couple of retired nurses. He probably thought she would have enough in common with them to keep a conversation going without him. He turned to her, smiled, and said, "Will you excuse me a minute, sweetheart? I need to talk business with someone. I know that sort of thing bores you." He smiled with effortless, condescending charm. "I'll catch up with you later."

She was still bristling over being treated as "the little woman" when he vanished into the crowd.

Forty minutes later, Raz was nowhere in sight when her hostess came and dragged her out of the corner where she was hiding with the single glass of wine she'd allowed herself.

"You haven't met my Harry yet, have you?" Livvy shouted at Sara as they passed close to one of the huge stereo speakers set up at the east end of the enormous living area. Livvy apparently liked New Age music. At least, that's what Sara thought it was. She'd never listened to harps and water sounds played at quite such decibels before. "I haven't seen that husband of yours around lately. He's probably out in the museum, looking at Harry's collection. They know better than to sneak off like that, both of 'em. You two have a fight?" she asked abruptly.

"Yes." That, at least, was true.

Livvy shook her head. "Men," she shouted fondly. "They're idiots, every blessed one of 'em."

Sara couldn't help smiling over the instant, partisan support. They circled two of the guests who were either arguing or agreeing at the tops of their lungs about something to do with naturalized shrubs. Or maybe it was naturalized citizens. One man—she was pretty sure it was a man—wore leather, ear studs and a nose ring. The other wore a clerical collar beneath his tailored suit jacket.

Those two were typical of the widely varied group that mobbed Livvy's home. Once Sara had stepped inside and seen her fellow guests, she'd stopped worrying about what she wore. Nothing short of total nudity would look out of place here.

When they turned a corner into the wide hallway, the noise level dropped to a more bearable level. Sara breathed deeply in relief.

"Is the music too loud?" Livvy asked.

"Oh, no. That is, I suppose it's just right for many people."

"It's too loud." Livvy shook her head. The shiny red and green balls that swung from her ears looked like they'd been borrowed from her Christmas tree. With them she wore tight pants in emerald green satin and a flowing white poet's shirt— an outfit that put her about midway between the poles of stuffy and outlandish established by her guests. "I wish someone would tell me when it gets turned up too high. I'm mostly deaf in one ear," she explained. "Burst eardrum. Never go scuba diving with an ear infection, Sara. Big mistake. Do you mind waiting here for a minute while I adjust the volume? Great. I'll be right back," she called over her shoulder as she disappeared through the door to the huge living room.

Sara glanced around. The hall she stood in was as wide as her little living room back in Houston, the carpet thick enough to swallow some of the noise pouring from the adjacent living room, the walls studded with doorways and hung with beautiful paintings.

She sipped at her wine and wandered down the hall, looking at beauty. She was smiling at an especially lovely watercolor of the ocean when the sound of feminine laughter nearby made her turn her head.

Raz came out of the nearest doorway.

He wasn't alone.

At some point that evening, Sara had met the blond woman attached to Raz's side, but no name floated up to the surface of her mind now. The woman wore a two-piece black outfit made of some material as clingy as she was. She was carrying a silky shawl in one hand—the hand that wasn't on Raz's chest. Her face was tilted up so that her long hair spilled enticingly over her bare shoulders and down her back. Her lips were moist and parted, as if she'd just licked them.

Or just been kissed.

Sara's mind went blank. For a second, so did Raz's face.

Then he smiled, but it was the wrong smile. Eddie MacReady would have smiled like that under similar circumstances—cocky, smug, a little bit mean. Not Raz. "You met Brenda earlier, didn't you?" he asked.

Words rose in Sara's throat, words so angry and confused she thought she would choke on them. The blonde was smiling at her, curving those moist, puffy lips to show a row of square white teeth. Sara couldn't speak past all those words. She nodded once, stiffly.

"Brenda isn't feeling well," Raz said, his eyes intent on Sara's. "She asked me if I would drive her home."

"Home?" she managed to repeat. Surely he couldn't mean

what he seemed to mean. He wouldn't go off with that toothy creature and leave her here.

He was still smiling Eddie's tight, mean smile at her. "You don't have to interrupt your fun, sweetheart. I'll be back soon enough. You stay here and have a good time."

Stay here. Yes, she realized, a sick feeling spreading in her stomach and lumping up in her throat. He was going to leave, but he wanted her to stay tucked away safely at the party, while he went and did things with the barracuda…things she'd wanted him to do with her.

What right had she to protest? He'd made her no promises. Sara swallowed, but the words that were lodged in her throat didn't go away, so she didn't speak.

His eyes narrowed as if she had argued. "You will stay here?"

She nodded. When he put his arm around the blond barnacle, Sara turned away, pretending to study the painting. But she felt them pass. Her mouth went dry, and her heart pounded as if she'd been in actual, physical danger. She felt vaguely nauseous.

For a moment she was tempted to put her hand out and stop him. She should tell him he had no business doing this to her. Whether she had any claim on him or not, all these people thought she did. He'd seen to that. But the thought of being rejected again while the barracuda watched and smirked made her sick. She didn't move. She just stood there while Raz and Brenda vanished into the living room, stood there and hated herself for being a coward.

A moment later, Livvy came out. "You still here?" she said, puzzled. "I could have sworn I saw Raz leaving the house just now. He was too far across the room for me to see clearly, but he—" Abruptly she stopped speaking.

Livvy's changing expression telegraphed her thoughts so precisely Sara might have laughed if she'd had any room left in her for amusement. Livvy had obviously seen Raz with a woman she had assumed, from the posture of the two people, was his new wife.

Sara turned away from the painting and tried for dignity, since she couldn't manage pride or courage. "He had to take someone home who wasn't feeling well."

Livvy looked entirely dubious. When she opened her mouth—no doubt to point out the weakness of Raz's excuse—Sara rushed into speech. "Please. I really can't discuss it, except to say he isn't...there are circumstances you don't know about."

Shrewd blue eyes narrowed on Sara. "There's something going on here that the two of y'all haven't told me about, isn't there?"

Sara didn't answer.

Livvy sighed. "Why is everyone convinced I can't keep a secret? Have I told Harry what I'm getting him for Christmas? Dropped a hint or two, maybe—but I haven't *told* him. C'mon now, honey, you need to meet my Harry," she said firmly, putting her hand on Sara's arm. "He'll cheer you up."

They found Harry presiding over his collection, just as Livvy had said, but the "museum" where he kept that collection was a garage.

Not any ordinary garage, however. It was a scrubbed and spotless concrete expanse large enough for four cars, but holding only a single sedan. All sorts of tools hung from pegboards along the walls.

The rest of the room was taken up by the motorcycles. Lots and lots of motorcycles.

Two men were admiring an elderly motorcycle with an attached sidecar that made Sara think of old black-and-white war movies. A third man sat on the floor beside the motorcycle, a short man with muscle-man shoulders, a pot belly and an exuberant salt-and-pepper mustache. He wore navy blue dress slacks and a soft knit shirt, and he held a wrench in one hand. An assortment of parts were scattered nearby.

"Harry," Livvy said reproachfully. "You promised."

He beamed up at her, his bald head round and shiny in the

overhead lights. He reminded Sara of a cross between a gnome and a circus strongman. "Just showing Jason the clutch."

Livvy sighed a wife's patient sigh. "Harry, I've brought Sara to meet you."

"Raz's Sara?" Harry set his wrench aside and stood. He wasn't much taller than she was, but his shoulders were twice as wide as hers. "Sara—" he said. There was a trace of something exotic in his speech, an accent she couldn't identify. But it made her think of Gypsies. He took one of her hands in both of his. "I am very glad to meet you. Do you like motorcycles?"

Brenda's choice of vehicles was as predictable as her behavior, once she and Raz were alone. She handed him the keys to a flashy little two-seater, and as soon as they slid inside, her busy hands could have caused a more easily distracted driver to miss any number of stop signs and other hazards.

A few minutes later Raz pulled up in front of one of the time-share condos nearby and tried to remember why he was there.

The hand on his thigh slid a little higher. Brenda leaned across the gearshift. Her breast brushed his arm. "Know what?" she breathed in his ear.

Oh, yeah. That's right. He was here to hurt Sara. So she'd get over whatever stupid-crazy crush she'd decided to have on him, because Sara, sweet, strong, foolish Sara, deserved better, one hell of a lot better, than him.

He, on the other hand, deserved exactly the sort of woman who was breathing in his ear. If he could manage to have her, that is. That was the other reason he was here. To find out if he was cured, with someone who wouldn't expect anything more from him than a quick, hard ride.

"What, sweetheart?" he murmured, his hand leaving the gearshift to move automatically to her waist, then up along her side. The silky material of her top slid up with his moving hand, leaving her middle exposed.

He knew where she wanted his hand. *Not yet*, he thought. He'd begin what he came here for in a minute. Just…not yet.

"I'm feeling much, much better." Her lips were near, very near. Her breath smelled like the mint lozenges he'd seen in her purse when she gave him her keys. "But I'm still a bit dizzy. Maybe you can help me with that."

"I've got a little problem you could help me with, too." He sure hoped she could, but the memory of Sara's face hung in the darkness of the car between them like a ghost.

"Is that so?" She took his hand from her side and pushed it up under her shirt, cupping it over her bare breast. "Does this help at all?"

Brenda was just his type, wasn't she? Firm breasts, hard nipples and no morals. She was obviously hot and ready, and every bit as empty as he was. He'd find out soon enough just how ready, he thought, and tried to feel interested. When that didn't work, he decided to get so close no ghosts could get between them.

He turned his head and kissed her.

Eight

"**A**nd this one," Harry said as he led her down the line of vintage motorcycles, "is a 1965 Harley-Davidson Panhead. A real prize. You see how the rocker-box cover is shaped?" He pointed at something chrome and shiny beneath the seat of the huge hog, proud as a new father. "I had that custom-made. Couldn't find one anywhere in decent shape. Some of the chrome is original, though. Look at this mousetrap." He pointed at another mysterious chrome part.

"It's—very shiny." She took a tiny sip of her wine to give herself something to do.

"Now, you sit on it. See how it feels."

"Oh, no, I couldn't. I don't know anything about motorcycles. I might let it fall over or something." It looked awfully heavy.

One of the two men who'd been admiring the ancient Army-issue motorcycle laughed. "Take him up on it, honey. Harry doesn't let just anyone touch one of his darlings, much less sit on it."

Harry smiled so widely he looked like a mustachioed Man In The Moon. "I had the stand custom-made to hold the bike upright. It can't fall over."

Harry's shiny-eyed expectation was as hard to refuse as a child's, but Sara hated to be conspicuous. She shook her head.

"You may as well humor him," Livvy said. "You can't fall over. Climbing on might be difficult, though, if your calf muscles are acting up." She turned to the man who'd called the motorcycles "Harry's darlings." He was well over six feet, with a beard, an earring and arms that were wider around than Sara's thighs. "Jason, give her a lift up, will you?"

Sara disliked the idea of a stranger helping her, even more than she disliked looking awkward. "No," she said quickly. "I can do it."

She handed Harry her cane and her wineglass. The motorcycle was very wide, with all sorts of pipes and footrests and things sticking out. She studied it for a moment, figuring out the best way to climb aboard. Then she moved.

By gripping the handlebar she could take some of her weight on that arm when she swung her right leg over. Fortunately, her skirt was long and full enough that she accomplished the maneuver without a serious loss of modesty. She put both hands on the handlebars, feeling foolish and vaguely daring.

"I've got to get back to our other guests, Harry," Livvy said. "You do remember that we're having a party? Raul, I'm sure I saw your wife looking for you..."

Sara stopped listening. She was looking at her hands on the grips. There was a ring on her left hand, a lying golden circle Raz had put there to fool his friends. He claimed to be good at lies. He hadn't bothered to lie to her, though, had he? He'd told her the truth when he said she couldn't expect anything from him except, maybe, a quick tumble. He'd left the party with another woman, tossing her an explanation so transparently false it was more of an insult than a genuine lie.

No, he certainly wasn't trying to deceive her.

Yet he'd looked like Eddie, not Raz, when he smiled. Eddie

was a role. A cover identity. Why had he needed to play a role if he was telling the truth?

Sara wanted to think he'd been lying, by his deeds if not by his words, when he left, but surely that was wishful thinking. Why would he lie? What reason would he have to pretend he was going to go to bed with Brenda the Barracuda if that wasn't exactly what he meant to do?

She was still caught in the riddle when Harry's voice recalled her to her surroundings. "What do you think, Sara? You want to try starting it? It's very easy. This model they made with both kick start and electronic ignition."

"Start it?" She blinked and looked around. She and Harry were alone. "Where did everyone go?"

"Livvy hauled Jason and Raul out of here with her. She had the idea you didn't want a lot of company. Now, you want to play with my toy, yes? First I'll double-check that it's in neutral." He did things with levers in different places, then put a key in the ignition. "Now," he said, pointing first at a dial on the center panel. "Turn the ignition to the right two clicks."

Why not? Sara turned the dial, most of her attention still snagged by the puzzle of Raz. He had kissed her like he wanted her, hadn't he? He'd put his hands on her, too, but he'd said it didn't mean anything. He'd told her not to expect anything, not even more kisses.

"Now you push the starter button, there on the right grip. That's all there is to it. This lady doesn't need much coaxing."

Sara pushed the black button. The motor caught immediately, and it was *noisy.*

"Hey," she said, startled out of her unhappy thoughts. The motorcycle vibrated beneath her like some huge, contented beast with a purr loud enough to wake the dead. Sara sat still, concentrating on absorbing the new experience.

"You've never been on a motorcycle?"

She shook her head. The vibration, the noise, the sense of constrained power, were…different. Interesting.

"You like it?" Harry beamed at her, speaking loudly to be

heard over the cycle. "Get that husband of yours to bring you over tomorrow. I don't let just anyone borrow one of my ladies, but for Raz and you I'll make an exception. He can take the Sportster, take you for a little ride."

"Thank you, but I don't think that will work out." She looked down at the handlebars, acutely aware of the lie she wore on her finger.

"Now, now." He reached out and shut off the ignition. The sudden silence was as startling as the noise had been. "Something is wrong. I don't know what, don't need to know, but a pretty girl like you shouldn't look so sad on her honeymoon. You two should come here tomorrow, take a ride together. You can't leave your troubles behind, no, but the wind in your face can blow a lot of the cobwebs out of your brain. Maybe blow some of the nonsense out of him, too." He smiled brightly.

She looked down. "I can't do this."

His smile faded.

"Not the motorcycle. Not that. You and Livvy are so nice, and I—" She sighed and looked straight at him, sick of pretense. "Raz isn't my husband. I'm not supposed to tell anyone that, but he isn't. He's my bodyguard."

His eyebrows went up. "You need a bodyguard?"

"I'm a witness to a multiple shooting." It was a relief, a vast relief, to let the story tumble out of her. She told him how she came to hire Raz and why they were on the island, pretending to be married. And as she talked she wondered how Raz had been able to stand living a lie for months at a time while undercover.

"Amazing." Harry's eyes were bright with curiosity. "I can understand why Raz didn't want my Livvy to know. She's a blessing I don't deserve, Livvy is. A marvelous woman. But there are no caution lights between her mind and her mouth. What she thinks, she says. So." He nodded, apparently in full agreement with himself. "You two will come for your ride tomorrow right after lunch, I think. One-thirty?"

She was baffled. "But I just told you—"

"What you told me doesn't change the fact that the two of you are having troubles."

"There isn't a 'two of us.'"

"Of course there is. This island is his sanctuary. A family place. You think Raz would have brought you here if you were no more than a client to him?"

"His brother's wife is involved, like I said. At least, she could be."

"No, no, that would be reason enough to take the job, maybe. Not reason enough to bring you to a family place. My Livvy, she has known the Rasmussins many years now, and she tells me what she knows. The father was a police officer until he retired. Both his sons are cops—something that makes him so proud he bursts his buttons sometimes. And they all come here to heal from their jobs. They don't bring their jobs with them. Yet Raz brought you here."

"I think he had reasons to come here that have nothing to do with me." Reasons or demons. Demons that had followed him ever since something happened to put him in the hospital.

"You believe that, don't you?" He patted her hand. "We'll see. Now I will teach you to shift gears. It's easy. This is the clutch. Hold it in with your left hand…yes, very good. The lever by your foot is the gearshift. I will show you first, then you try it. Like this…"

Sara didn't know why she went along with him. Partly, she supposed, because there was something terribly reassuring about Harry's bossiness. She thought that being bossed around by a favorite brother or uncle must feel something like this. And her shyness wasn't an issue with Harry. She didn't have to think of things to say, because he handled the conversation just fine all by himself.

Except for her vague daydreaming about Eddie MacReady, who didn't really exist, Sara had spent very little time on fantasy. Sitting on a big, black machine and learning how to take it through its gears was so alien to her idea of who and what she was that she forgot to be self-conscious.

She almost forgot who Raz had left with. And why.

"You have a good touch," Harry said approvingly as she went from third to fourth gear. "You like playing with my big, shiny toy?"

"As long as it isn't moving." She shook her head. "Do you know what we call toys like yours in the ER?"

"Donor cycles?" He chuckled. "I have heard the term. But, of course, I always wear a helmet. So will you, tomorrow, when you and Raz come for your ride. You can wear your own jeans, but you will borrow one of Livvy's leather jackets for protection. Do you have boots?"

Some of her pleasure faded. "Harry," she said, "Raz and I are just pretending to have a…a relationship. He isn't going to bring me here for a ride."

"Oh, yes? Pretending, are you? And I suppose you are only pretending to be sad because he went off with some woman and left you here?"

Her hand slipped, popping the clutch.

Harry shook his head reproachfully. "That is no way to treat a fine machine. If the engine had been on, you would have shot forward, splat! Right into the wall."

"I'm sorry." She stared at the handlebars. "How did you know about Raz leaving?"

"Livvy told me while you were thinking your sad thoughts. She is worried because she likes Raz very much, and such behavior is unlike him. So, because Livvy worries, and because I like you, I will fix things." He nodded confidently.

Sara's hands tightened on the grips. "I don't want to talk about this."

"Of course not. You think it's none of my business. That's okay," he assured her, patting her arm. "You don't have to tell me what you feel. For one thing, I already know. But you should tell Raz. Young men are not smart like me. You have to tell them everything. But before you can tell him what you feel, you must know this for yourself."

"Not much mystery there," she muttered. Lust was not a subtle emotion. She sighed and lifted her leg to climb off the motorcycle. Her hip was stiff, and her calf tingled when she put her weight on it, warning that it was still not trustworthy. "Would you pass me my cane, please?"

He handed it to her.

"Thank you."

"You are wishing I hadn't said anything."

She managed a smile. "I enjoyed playing with your toy, Harry, but I think I've had enough partying for now." What she wanted more than anything was to go home to her own little house, but home was far away and no longer safe. "Would you make my excuses to Livvy? I think I'll head back to the cottage now."

After all, Javiero had probably never even heard of Mustang Island. There was no point in her staying obediently at the party until Raz came back. She didn't want to deal with him in public. She didn't want anyone else noticing how miserable she was.

"Of course I will tell her. After I take you home. We will ride the Springer, I think. It's a two-up, very comfortable for the passenger. You see it in the corner over there, the big road bike with the fringed saddlebags?"

"But I don't—"

"You'll need some pants," he went on, looking her over critically. "That skirt is no protection. Livvy will find you something."

"Harry—"

"Do you have a key to the house?"

She opened her mouth, then closed it, feeling stupid. No, Raz had the key, which meant she had little choice about remaining here. She would have to face him in a roomful of people when he returned from being with that woman.

Anger stirred, sluggish and dark, deep inside. How dare he put her in this position? "No key," she said, her jaw tight.

"No problem." Harry smiled happily. "I have a key. The Rasmussins left one with us long ago so we could keep an eye on things. So, now we will get you some warm clothes. Then we will let the wind blow the cobwebs out of your brain, so you can figure out for yourself that you're in love with your pretend husband.'' He beamed at her. ''Do not be too hard on him. All young men are foolish.''

The wind was cold when it whipped by at thirty or forty miles an hour, numbing Sara's face below the helmet's visor. The noise of wind and cycle deafened her in spite of the helmet. She held on tightly to the man in front of her, leaning with him as the motorcycle roared down the curving shore road, slowing as they reached the houses on the edge of town.

They slowed still more as they pulled into the circular drive. Harry eased to a stop right next to the porch steps, and Sara climbed off. Her movements were stiff, but the tingling in her calf had eased and she no longer had a skirt getting in her way. She'd exchanged it for a pair of Livvy's jeans. They were much too big, of course, as was the leather jacket Harry had insisted she wear.

She pulled her helmet off and listened to the sighing of the ocean.

''Here you go, my dear.'' Harry handed her her cane, which he'd worn stuck in his belt, slanted across his back diagonally, like a samurai's sword. ''Did you like your ride?''

They'd gone the wrong way. Harry had taken her up the coastal road for several miles before turning around and coming back. ''You are a bossy and manipulative man, Harry.'' And wrong, too. He might have been right about her enjoying a ride on his motorcycle, but he was wrong about everything else. She couldn't be stupid enough to have fallen for a heartbreaker like Raz.

''It is part of my charm.'' Harry wore black leather and a dark blue helmet that looked black in the yellow glow of the porch light. The strongman side of his personality was more obvious when he was on his motorcycle, but the elf was still evident in his smile.

She handed him her helmet. ''I enjoyed the ride,'' she admitted.

''Good.'' He turned to fasten the helmet behind him. ''You will come tomorrow?''

"I don't think so."

"You make it difficult for me to fix things," he said severely.

She had to smile. "There's nothing to fix."

He sighed. "I have not yet blown out all the cobwebs, I see. You are a stubborn young woman. I don't—what is it?" He twisted around.

Sara was staring over his shoulder at the sporty little car that pulled up in front of the cottage. The passenger door opened, making the interior light come on and flooding the night with the driving beat of some hard rock group. Sara had a clear view of the two people in the car. The tip of Brenda's cigarette glowed brightly as she took a deep drag.

The second Raz shut the door, the little car peeled away from the curb.

Raz's face was a blur in the darkness. Yet Sara felt it when his gaze locked with hers, felt it as surely as if she'd touched him, or he had touched her. Her heartbeat was a distinct throb in her throat. She pressed her hand there, as if she would contain that relentless beat with her fingers.

Contain it? How could she contain anything? She felt too much. Anger. Wind. The cold undertow of fear, and the subtle bite of the graveled drive she stood on. Humiliation and the air both tasted salty, like the sea she heard breathing nearby. Deep inside she knew the pull of that slow rhythm, a tugging as steady and certain as fate, flooding her with confusion.

Raz started toward her.

"Well," Harry said, lowering his visor, "it must be time for me to go home."

How long has Raz been gone? Sara asked herself. It was a stupid question, of course. Sex didn't have to take long at all. "Thank you for the ride, Harry."

"You are welcome." He backed up his motorcycle with a few pushes from his short legs, turned it, then gave it enough gas to pull out of the driveway. He didn't stop to speak to the man walking slowly toward Sara.

All at once she didn't want to face Raz. She wanted to be

inside, to close the door of her bedroom behind her and try to close the door on the feelings flooding her. Sara hurried up the four steps that led to the porch, taking out the key Harry had given her earlier.

Nerves and haste made her jam the key in the lock wrong. She was jiggling it frantically when his hand slammed onto the door near her head. He stood close behind her, his voice low and intense in her ear, his body so close she felt its heat. ''What the hell do you think you're doing?''

Her heart pounded. She felt dizzy. ''I think that's obvious.''

''You little fool. You weren't supposed to leave the party. You agreed to that.''

''I changed my mind.'' From somewhere she found the nerve—or the need—to look at him over her shoulder. ''What can it possibly matter?''

''You ask that when you know there's a punk who wants nothing more than to kill you?'' His lips were thin with anger, his eyes dark with feelings every bit as volatile as her own. The sight should have restored her to reason.

It didn't. ''Javiero is in Houston.''

''You received a letter from him telling you that, maybe? Postmarked from Houston?'' He put his hands on her shoulders. ''Get out of the way. And unless you're ready to fire me here and now, you will do as I say from now on. Stay out here until I tell you it's safe to come in.''

He moved her. She had little choice but to give way, to stand aside and watch as he unlocked the door and swung it open. It infuriated her. She hated being weak. She wanted to grab him, to make him listen, make him—what? What did she want?

Raz unjammed the key, unlocked the door, but left it closed while he reached inside his jacket. The gun he withdrew was a matte black that offered no giveaway gleam.

He swung the door open. A flash of motion near their feet made Sara's heart leap into her throat. But it was only Mac, bolting out the door and across the porch to freedom.

Sara's heart was still thudding wildly when Raz disappeared into the darkened house.

She was sure there was no danger. In spite of the way her hand went to her throat, in spite of the bounding pulse that urged her to either follow him or flee, her mind held her firmly in place. Reason told her there was no danger, because Javiero was in Houston.

And if, against all odds, there had been danger, reason also told her she would only be in Raz's way if she followed. Sara was too used to dealing in grim truths to evade one, however unpalatable she found it. So she stayed on the porch, anger and fear simmering together in an unhealthy stew. The fear was familiar. Sara had dealt with that all her life and knew she could ignore it if she had to. But she didn't like being angry. That he could make her feel an emotion she tolerated so poorly only increased her anger.

One by one, lights came on inside. Yet Sara's fear didn't diminish. Unwanted, unreasonable, it continued to bubble in her. Then Raz appeared in the doorway as quietly as he'd vanished. "It's clear," he said curtly.

Sara intended to go straight to her room. That's what she meant to do, yet when she followed him inside she went to the center of the big room and stood there, motionless, while he locked the front door and hung his sports jacket on the coat tree. She watched him unfasten his shoulder holster with its deadly contents and hang that up, too. She didn't speak or think. She just watched as he turned, watched the smooth muscles in his thighs working with beautiful efficiency beneath the worn fabric of his jeans as he started toward her.

"What are you staring at?" he demanded.

"I don't know." That was the chilling truth. She didn't know what sort of man he was. Her feelings said one thing, while his actions shouted something else.

"It's time we got a few things straight." He stopped in front of her, his eyes cold as he grabbed her arm. "You can fire me, or you can do as you're told. No more tagging after me down to the beach, or leaving a place I've determined is safe, or—"

"Don't touch me." Her jaw ached with her anger, with the need to keep it tamped down.

His grip tightened enough that, even through the bulky sleeve of her borrowed jacket, she felt each finger clearly. "What in the hell were you thinking of, getting Harry to bring you home? Did it occur to you that you could be exposing him to danger?"

She jerked her arm out of his grip. "You left! You weren't there, so I figured the decisions were up to me. So I told him the truth about us, and he offered to bring me home."

"You *what?*"

"I told Harry the truth." Fear still had her by the throat— stupid, irrational, pointless fear—while anger made her pulse pound. Because she didn't know what else to do, she started for her bedroom. "Don't worry. He understands that he can't tell anyone. He agreed to that." She moved much more slowly than she wanted. Her leg felt weak and tricky.

Like her heart?

No, she thought, panicked. No, her heart wasn't involved. Her body and her pride, yes—he affected both of them strongly, but that was all. This terrible fear flooding her had nothing to do with her heart. She was afraid because… because…

"I don't believe this," he said. "Are you determined to ruin any chance I have of keeping you alive? Are you so childish you would endanger yourself to satisfy a fit of temper?"

She stopped. "Don't you dare call me childish. You're the one who left. If I'm in such danger, why did you leave me at that party so you could—so you could—you're supposed to be protecting me, but you left!"

His expression was ugly, as ugly as the feelings choking her. "I left so I could screw Brenda. Go ahead and say it. Or are you too saintly to use that sort of language?"

Tears of rage blurred her vision. "You humiliated me.

Everyone there thought we were newly married, and you went off with that toothy barracuda clinging to you. You had no right to do that."

"I had every right. You employ me, you don't own me, and a couple of kisses don't entitle you to my body."

She screeched and threw her cane at him.

It was a lousy toss, not really meant to connect. The cane clattered to the floor near his feet without touching him. He stared at it, astonished.

Blood and anger alike drained from Sara's head so fast she feared she might faint. "Oh, no." She shook her head. "No, I didn't mean it. I'm sorry. I didn't mean—" From deep inside her rose the sound of voices. Loud, angry voices. "No," she whispered.

He frowned. "Sara?" He started toward her. "What's wrong?"

"I'm sorry." She couldn't be touched, not now. She was too near some cliff, some dreadful point from which one wrong step would send her falling and falling. "W-we'll talk later. Tomorrow." She turned—too quickly. Her leg, her damned weak leg, betrayed her by buckling.

He was close enough to step forward and catch her up against him, his arms strong and steady. "What is it? You're pale as a ghost. Is it your leg? Your hip?"

She shook her head wildly.

"Please," he said, his hands gentle as he turned her to face him. "Tell me what's wrong, sweetheart."

But all she could do was repeat, "I didn't mean it."

"What didn't you mean?"

"I don't yell. I don't argue. I...I can't."

He smiled, but his eyes worried over her. "You were doing a pretty decent job of it a minute ago."

"You don't understand. Anger makes me ill. Loud, angry voices..." She heard them again, screaming out of the depths of her memory, two angry people taking each other apart. And she couldn't stand it.

"They were fighting," she whispered, her hands closing on

his forearms with desperate strength. "Just before our car crossed the divider. They were angry and they were yelling, and that's why he—that's why—" She closed her eyes, but she couldn't close off any part of the memory now. She heard it, felt it, saw it—the angry voices, the little bump as they went over the divider—and the headlights, coming straight at them.

"Sara." Strong arms closed around her, pulling her against him again. He felt like safety and warmth and life. She needed him. She needed… "They told me I was trapped in the wreck for two hours," she whispered. "But I don't remember that. I just remember the voices, the arguing. And the headlights."

One of his arms banded her waist beneath the borrowed leather jacket. His other hand stroked her hair. "You break my heart, you know that?"

No, it was the other way around. With every touch he undid her. She wrapped her arms around him and held on, turning her head so that her cheek lay over his heart. She couldn't hear his heartbeat clearly, not with the thickness of his shirt between them, but she felt it the same way she had felt the pull, earlier, of the ocean. Between one beat and the next, the unheard rhythm of his heart drew the truth from hers.

She was in love.

Sara closed her eyes and held on. It was all she could think of to do.

Raz's hand lingered at the nape of her neck, kneading gently for several moments before he spoke. "Do you want to tell me about the accident?"

Unwillingly, her eyes came open again. "Do you really want to hear?"

"I rather think I want whatever you will give me."

His words sent a little thrill through her, half fear, half… something more dangerous. "We were on vacation," she said softly. "Daddy had stayed up the night before working on a brief, and Mother was angry about that. She didn't like sharing him with his work, and especially not on vacation. She…well, some people need more attention than others, just like some plants need more sunshine. She and Daddy loved each other. I do believe that. But sometimes—sometimes she was demanding, and sometimes he was distant, and then they would argue.''

His hand rested, warm and reassuring, at her nape. He said, ''Anger can kill. When people don't respect the rules of civilization and violence erupts, anger can be deadly. But people manage to argue all the time without fatal consequences, sweetheart. And constantly swallowing your anger can kill, too. It just happens more slowly.''

At some point her hand had begun tracing little patterns on his back. The feel of him soothed her. She even smiled slightly. ''I do remember them saying something of the sort in medical school. But knowing why I can't abide anger and changing the way I react to it are two different things.''

''I can understand that.''

Sara didn't believe in hiding, but it was hard, very hard, to bring up the next thing. ''I know I don't have any right to be angry over who you take to bed, not as things stand between us. But you've given me some pretty mixed messages, Raz. You haven't been fair.''

He gave a short, mirthless laugh. ''That's the understatement of the decade.'' A subtle tension invaded his body. He moved both hands to her waist and pulled back. When there was a bit of distance between them, when she was looking up at his face, her hands resting on his forearms, he spoke. ''I didn't take Brenda to bed.''

She shook her head, surprised and relieved. Vastly relieved. ''You changed your mind?''

His face, with those creases that folded together so intriguingly when he smiled, looking worn and tired now. ''No. I intended to go through with it. You've got to let go of this damn fool idea you have about me as some kind of good guy. Tonight should have shown you how far off base that notion is.''

Tonight he'd held her, comforted her through a visit from

her personal nightmare. What was that supposed to show her? "Then Brenda changed her mind."

His grin flickered. "No, she was mad as hell when things didn't go the way she expected. Didn't you notice the way she peeled out of here?"

"Then why—?"

"Because I couldn't."

He said it flatly, but Sara's mind still didn't absorb his meaning for a long moment. Then her mouth formed an *O* of surprise. She spoke before she thought. "That's ridiculous."

The corner of his mouth turned up, but his eyes stayed bleak. "There are some people who might consider it a pretty good joke on me, all right, but I hadn't thought someone as tender-hearted as you would be one of them."

Raz was hurting. Badly. She wanted to wrap herself around him and make the pain go away, but she had no idea what to do, what to say. He needed someone like Brenda, she thought. Someone who understood a man's physical needs. Not a desperately uncertain near-virgin.

But she *was* a doctor. Belatedly, her training came to her rescue. "You weren't drinking, so that's not the problem. However, there are numerous possible physical causes, from diabetes to, rarely, certain tumors. Have you seen a doctor?"

He looked bemused. "No, but—"

"Are you taking any regular medications? Blood pressure medicine, diuretics in particular, can make it difficult to sustain an erection. Certain antidepressants have been known to inhibit sexual function, as well."

A hint of color reddened his cheeks. "Did anyone ever tell you you had a way with words?"

"No."

"Good. You don't."

Now she flushed. Her hands clenched on his arms. "I don't know any other way to talk about this. And it *is* important to rule out physical causes."

"I know the reason for my problem just as surely as you know why anger upsets you."

She bit her lip. "But you should still get an examination. Just to be sure."

"Sara," he said, and there was actually a smile in his eyes now, "if you'll let me put your hand where I want it, you could confirm—firsthand, so to speak—that my problem isn't physical."

She blinked. "You mean you, ah—"

"Oh, yes," he said, and his voice dropped lower, into a husky, intimate range. Sara's breath caught as the change in his voice, in his eyes, carried her into heady new territory. "I want you, Sara."

"I...don't know what to say."

He smiled. "Leave that to me." His hands moved. With one smooth motion, he slid the oversize jacket from her shoulders. It fell to the floor.

Her breath caught.

"I've wanted to do that all evening. That, and other things." His hands slid up her arms to her shoulders and started down her body. They skimmed the sides of her breasts, pausing just above her waist. "You see, every time I'm around you, my problem seems to go away. I've tried to keep my hands off you, Sara. I don't want to use you. But it feels so good...to feel. Do you have any idea how good it can be just to *feel?*"

Yes, her heart and her eyes said. Yes, she knew.

Slowly his hands moved up from her waist. "I feel alive when I touch you," he said, and spread his fingers so that their tips brushed the bottom curve of her breasts. His hands moved up slowly—so very slowly—until they closed over her breasts.

She gasped.

"I want to keep touching you," he said, and he rubbed fire through her skin into her blood with his clever hands while he watched her face. "But surely you have better sense than to let me do the things I want to do...like removing the rest of your clothes, one by one. Because once I get you naked, I won't stop. I'll enjoy you slowly, pretty Sara, with my mouth and my eyes and my hands...if you let me."

His hands moved away for a moment, and she almost cried out at the loss. Then he unfastened the first button of her sweater.

"Raz," she said, and clutched his wrists, so unsteady she thought she might fall.

"Should I stop, Sara?" he said, and he slid the next button through the buttonhole. Her sweater gaped open. "Tell me to stop."

Sara looked into his eyes and she knew her feelings must be obvious. Her blood sang a wild song to her, inviting her as surely as were his hands and his hooded, haunted eyes to a dance she didn't recognize and couldn't resist.

He needed her. It was enough. It would have to be enough. Her voice was calm when she spoke. "You know I don't want you to stop."

Nine

There were seven dainty white buttons on Sara's sweater. Raz's hands were trembling before he reached the last of them. It would be enough, he told himself, if he could touch her, hold her, bring her pleasure. It would, perhaps, have to be enough.

But oh, how he wanted to know her heat from the inside.

When he'd fumbled the last button from its buttonhole, he took the edges of her sweater and folded them back. In spite of the urgency in his blood, he smiled. Practical Sara wore a charmingly impractical wisp of white lace and silk over her breasts.

He put his hands at her waist and looked at her face. Embarrassed color highlighted her cheeks. There was uncertainty in her eyes—and something more. Something stronger than the flashfire of lust.

"Sara," he said, desperate and not sure why. He would hurt her, he knew that—sooner or later he would hurt her, and that was reason enough to be half-frantic with guilt. But he suspected the worst of his urgency was selfish, rising from the fear that she might still yet show enough sense to refuse him. "Sara, I'm a mess. I'm not offering you a future, not even the chance of a future. You do understand that?"

Her head moved in a tiny nod.

"And you want this, anyway?"

She must have found the smile he'd lost, because her lips turned up. "Oh, yes." Her eyes glowed with a woman's certainty and secrets. "But—there's just one thing."

"What?"

"I really think you should kiss me."

They were both smiling when he did that.

She tasted of wishes and wine, of midnight and the first faint promise of dawn. He wanted it all. He wanted everything. His mouth turned avid, eating at hers, telling her what he needed, what he had to have from her. She answered with a quick, startled gasp and eager hands that clutched his shoulders, then hurried to his chest, where they kneaded him like a cat. He started to pull her tight against him, but remembered that she'd nearly fallen earlier.

"I think," he told her softly, his mouth nibbling at hers between words, "that we need to get you off your feet, sweetheart. And I know just where I want you." He felt her smile against his lips. That small, subtle movement excited him more than Brenda's boldest gropings had.

He slid his arms beneath her and lifted carefully. His mouth never left hers as he carried her to his bedroom.

It was a plain room with white walls and white curtains, scuffed maple furniture and faded blue bedspreads on the two double beds. Years ago, it had held bunk beds and a train set. Eventually his father had taken the train set home with him.

There was something inexpressibly erotic about laying Sara down in the middle of so many memories.

She smiled up at him, and he thought he had never seen anything more perfect. Her hair was dark, her skin pale, her eyes blue like the bedspread, only smokier, hazed with desire. Her white sweater hung open, letting him look at creamy skin and that luscious scrap of lace that didn't quite hide her dark nipples. Her legs were restless.

So was he. He came down on the bed beside her, kissing her throat, letting his hands press and linger and tease. "Sweetheart," he said, lifting his head. "Is there anything I should know?" When she looked at him blankly, he said it plainly. "Are you a virgin?"

"Oh." She delighted him by blushing again. He could see exactly how far down the rosy color went, and he couldn't resist following that color with his mouth, tracing kisses along the edge of the wispy lace bra. "No, I..." She made a vague little sound of approval when he licked the lace. "I am a beginner, though."

"A beginner, huh?" He smiled and lifted his head again so he could unclasp her bra. At the sight of her breasts, round and lovely, needs swirled in him—the need to take, to possess, to rip the last bits of cloth from her body and thrust inside her. He inhaled sharply and lowered his head, determined to give Sara every breath of gentleness he possessed.

She nodded. "I..."

He kissed the underside of her breast. "Yes?"

"I'm something of a perfectionist," she said, her breath unsteady. "Once I decide to do something, I want to do it perfectly. When I tried this the first time, I wasn't very good at it, and I never—oh, my, that's—that feels so..."

"You never what, sweetheart?" His face was very near her nipple, which seemed to him to be pouting. "This needs a bit of attention, doesn't it?" he said, and licked it.

Her hands clenched in his hair. "Oh, yes, that...I like that."

"You never what?" he repeated, and blew on her damp nipple.

She shivered. "Never had anyone I wanted to practice this with before."

"Is that what we're doing?" He sent his hand wandering up her leg, her hip. "Practicing?"

"Well, *you* probably don't need to practice."

And yet this was new to him. Fearfully new. He'd never

seduced an innocent before. He'd never felt hunger like this, with talons that stretched all the way inside him and ripped him open when they flexed, letting the hunger spill out. Ruthlessly he forced that hunger back down again.

He propped himself up on one elbow and watched her expression as he spread his hand on her belly. She was so small, so deceptively delicate. His hand spanned her stomach with his fingertips resting on her mound. He wanted to put his hand between her legs, to rub her there. He wanted to get inside her quickly. Now.

His breath came quicker, harder, but he held himself in check as he moved his hand around to her hip. "And here?" he said, rubbing gently. "Should I know anything so I don't hurt you?" That particular pain, surely, he could spare her.

"I have...there are scars."

He shook his head. "That wasn't what I meant."

"I don't think anything we do could hurt," she said shyly. "Though maybe you shouldn't, um, rest all your weight on me. Raz..."

"Yeah?" Because he couldn't resist those pretty, pouty breasts any longer, he cupped one, lazily flicking his finger back and forth over the nipple.

"I...oh, my...I know you said you wanted to go slowly, and I know beginners usually learn more if they take things one step at a time, but...maybe we could focus on teaching me things another time."

Her hands slid up his chest, rubbing here, testing there, as if she needed the feel of him. His breath hissed between his teeth, and his muscles flexed in sharp, involuntary reaction to those questing hands. She seemed to like that. Her lips parted and her pupils were dark and luminous with pleasure. "Because I really don't feel like going slow," she whispered. "If you don't mind too much, I would like you to—hurry."

Raz grabbed for control. And missed. Hasty needs sent his mouth to hers, where he plundered. His hands sped over her body, molding, absorbing—stripping.

Shy? Had he thought his Sara was shy? She shed her timidity along with her clothes. The sound of fabric tearing as he dragged her sweater off incited them both to a race neither could lose. Sara obviously wanted him naked. Her hands, those beautiful, agile hands made that clear. But he couldn't pause to help her, couldn't slow down his own urgent need for her flesh.

Their hands collided. Their noses bumped as they sought another kiss, and another. Teeth ground together and seams ripped. Joy coiled itself up tightly in a tangled bliss of arms and thighs, hands and straining bodies. They rolled together on the bed, sending covers sliding to the floor in a frenzy of exploration. He barely retained enough sense to grab his wallet, and the protection it contained, from his pants before they hit the floor.

The taste of Sara behind her ear mixed with the darker flavors of the flesh on the inside of her thigh. Her flavors and his pleasure nearly exploded together when she bent herself double so that her avid mouth could skim down his stomach. In a smooth, instinctual seeking she traced a path that ended with the tip of her tongue testing him where he would have thought no beginner would venture.

But thoughts, like the ghosts from Raz's nightmares, were whipped into tatters by the storm between them. Automatically, instinctively, Sara ended up beneath him, her legs parted for his entry. Just as instinctively, he topped her body with his own. His hands were shaking when he rolled the condom on.

Then he cupped her slim hips in his hands, and thrust inside.

Her eyes shot open wide. Her hands fluttered on his shoulders in quick, urgent benedictions. And the universe paused for a breath, paused long enough for one thought to slide into his dazzled mind. A thought as long as a single word.

Home.

Then his body and hers took over. Eager for the heights where breath and sanity could both be lost and never missed, they moved together.

Some ragged cousin of Raz's usual control fingered his

mind. He remembered her hip and searched her face for any sign of discomfort. He saw eyes hazed with sensation, muscles tight with lust and damp with heat, a swollen, trembling mouth. Then her eyes met his and *knew* him—and he lost even the ghost of control. He thrust harder, quicker, and when she was gasping, grasping at him, begging with her body and with the soft, urgent sounds she made, he slipped his hand between them.

He watched when he sent her over, just as he had said he would. He watched the astonished pleasure overtake her as she convulsed beneath him and around him. Then his own climax rocked into him, a blow that knocked future into past, and both into oblivion.

Oblivion was a soft and nameless place. Sara drifted out of it a little at a time, coming back to herself as quietly as a leaf rocking its way from a branch to the ground. Just as the leaf's path is gentled by the unsteady currents of the air it glides on, so was hers eased by the still-unsteady breath of the man whose chest she rested on.

Raz had remembered what she'd said about his weight. Even in the mindlessness following climax he hadn't let himself rest all his weight on her. He'd rolled to his side, then to his back, taking her with him. They'd ended up with him underneath and her on top. He'd even grabbed the covers and dragged one corner of them over the two of them.

Sara smiled. She'd heard being on top could be fun.

He spoke, his voice husky and amused. "You're smiling."

"I'm happy." She drew her hand up on his chest with her so she could pet the muscles there. She'd been right, back when she thought of him as Eddy MacReady. He really did have a world-class chest.

"I was ready to apologize for losing it and getting so rough, but if you're smiling…"

"Were you rough?" she asked, curious. "It seemed just about right to me."

"It did, did it?" He chuckled. "I just wanted to be sure I

didn't hurt your hip. There are lots of other ways to make love. If any of them aren't comfortable, we'll just keep making our way down the list.'' Thoughtfully he added, ''It's a pretty long list.''

Relief made Sara giddy. Apparently he didn't think of this as the only time they would come together. She raised herself up on her forearms so she could see his face, and lifted one eyebrow. ''You've got a list?''

He smiled, his hands sliding up her back. ''I could come up with one.''

She raised a second eyebrow to go with the first. ''Really?'' Love, she thought, was like a lot of bogeymen. Once you faced it, named it, you simply couldn't be as frightened as you were when it remained locked up in the dark.

Not that it lacked teeth. At some point she expected she would feel those teeth, but not now. Now, her lover was smiling up at her, and Sara felt so much love overflowing her that it didn't matter if she was the only one who loved. And who knows? Maybe just a little of the love she floated on *did* come from him. ''And is a list all you can...come up with?''

He laughed. ''And to think I was convinced you were shy.''

I am, she wanted to say. With anyone else, she wouldn't even think such thoughts, much less speak them. But somehow, with Raz, she was different. Better. He'd needed her, and she hadn't failed him. He'd wanted her when he hadn't wanted anyone else.

She smiled. ''I'm learning.''

''Oh, yeah?'' He reached up to cup her breasts. ''That's another thing. I thought you were supposed to be a beginner.'' The gentle circular motion of his hands stirred something in the pit of Sara's stomach she could have sworn was sated and sleeping. ''Those were some pretty advanced moves you were putting on me, slim.''

''They were?'' Pleased, she shifted so she could run one hand up his chest. ''Which did you like best?''

''Well, there was that thing with your mouth and my, uh—''

She flushed scarlet. "Oh, well, I never—I just—it seemed like a good idea at the time."

He grinned. "It was a wonderful idea. An incredible idea. A super-duper splendiferous idea." But, a little at a time, his grin faded. His hands slid away from her breasts to rest at her waist. "But some of your ideas...this changes things."

"That's not a tone of voice I like hearing right now."

"I have to say this, sweetheart."

She wanted to go on playing. Touching. Being happy. But she hadn't really healed Raz by giving herself to him. Whatever demons haunted him might have been temporarily banished by passion, but they were already sneaking back. "All right."

He took a deep breath, as if he found this difficult to say. "You're going to have to get another bodyguard."

"What?" It was so different from anything she'd expected, it took her a moment to catch up with his meaning. "You mean—because you and I—because we went to bed together?"

"It's not the bed. It's what we did in the bed." His grin was a poor echo of the cocky expression she'd seen on his face so often, and it vanished all too quickly. "Sara, one of the first rules any cop, public or private, learns is not to get personally involved. A bodyguard whose attention stays below his belt because he's been taking his subject to bed puts them both in danger."

"I don't want someone else. I won't have anyone else."

He sighed. His hand slid down her side beneath the covers, pausing to rub her hip gently. He paid no more attention to the scars now than he had while making love to her. "I've crossed too many lines, Sara. I can't afford the consequences if something goes wrong because of it."

"Raz, do you really think you'll pay less attention to protecting me, now that you've been to bed with me?"

"My judgment is impaired. I proved that by taking you to bed."

That stung. "You're not being logical." She sat up, pulling

enough of the bedspread with her that she was at least covered from the waist down. "Didn't your brother want you for this job because he knew you would take it personally, because of your sister-in-law?"

"That's different."

"Why?" she asked, soft and fierce. "Why is it different? You can't have it both ways. You can't say that caring makes you try harder and then turn around and claim that caring makes you incompetent."

He was silent for a long moment, then said, "I hope you haven't gotten the wrong idea."

"What do you mean?"

He looked oddly helpless. "It's not that I don't care, Sara, but I'm not— We have no future."

She swallowed. "If you mean that you're not in love with me, I know that." It was easier, marginally, to say it herself than it would be to hear him say it. "But are you saying you don't care at all?"

He didn't say anything for a long moment. Then he sat up, took her face in his two hands and kissed her lightly on the lips. "You deserve a great deal better than me, little mouse."

"Now you're being absurd as well as illogical."

He shook his head. "I wish I knew how to tell you what you've done for me."

She smiled shyly. "I made you feel sexy."

"Very sexy."

"You made me feel that way, too."

His mouth dipped close for another kiss. "Did I?" He pressed kisses along a path up her cheek. "What am I making you feel now?"

"Warm."

"Really?" His mouth found a sensitive spot behind her ear. "How about now?" And his hands drifted down to cup her breasts.

"Awake." Her back arched involuntarily as he took her nipples between his thumbs and forefingers. "And...alert. Definitely alert."

"Is that so? Do you know, I seem to recall something you said earlier about taking things slow."

"I did?" His fingers were doing incredibly distracting things.

"Mmm-hmm. You thought we might try going slowly next time." He let go of her nipples and gave her one gentle push.

She fell backward on the bed, laughing. "Is it next time already?" Her hands reached for his shoulders as he bent over her—such lovely shoulders, firm and smooth-muscled and, for the moment, hers. For now he was hers to savor, to please…to love, though she couldn't say the word.

He took her hands and put them on the bed above her head. "My turn first," he murmured. His hands slid down her arms. "Be a good girl and hold real still. I want to see if I can make you feel one-tenth as good as you've made me feel."

She closed her eyes and let herself drift on the sensations. "As long as I get a turn, too." His hands skimmed over her breasts so lightly she shivered. His fingertips slid down her sides—lightly, lightly.

It tickled.

She twitched. He did it again. Her eyes flew open. "Don't you dare," she said.

"You're ticklish." He sounded delighted.

"A little." The gleam in his eyes made her frown at him. "You should bear in mind that I know a great deal about human anatomy."

His fingers drifted around to her front—where she wasn't ticklish, thank goodness. "Threatening me, are you?"

"Let's call it a promise. For example…" Feeling daring, she put one hand on his thigh and slid it upward. "I know where there are an incredible number of nerve endings." Boldly she cupped him. "We're supposed to be teaching me things, aren't we?"

The devil was in his eyes again—but she was pretty sure he wasn't thinking about tickling her this time. "Ah, but I told you to keep your hands over your head. That's a moving violation, you know."

"What?"

"I'm afraid I'm going to have to punish you," he said, taking her errant hand and putting it over her head again. With his other hand he drew the covers down. He took his time about looking her over, making appreciative sounds.

He was only playing. She knew that, yet she felt exposed and uncertain. "Raz—I really am a beginner, you know."

"I know," he said gently, and bent and pressed a kiss to her mouth. "I'm not going to do anything that makes you uncomfortable. Trust me?"

She met his eyes and gave him the only answer she could. "Yes."

For an instant his eyes were utterly serious. "I won't let you regret that, Sara. I promise." Then he looked at her body again, his eyes kindling, his mouth turning up in a devilish smile. "Now, where was I? Oh, yes. Right about…here." He bent to tickle her belly button with his tongue.

For a liar, Raz told the truth quite well. He took her on their second journey slowly and carefully, and she was quietly frantic for him when he finally slipped inside and took the ache away.

And she didn't regret it. Not any of it.

Hours later Sara drifted on a sweet tide that carried her between sleeping and waking. Normally she would have been up by now, having captured the six or so hours of sleep that were all she usually needed. But normally she wouldn't have been sleeping with a lover. Her lover.

Several times she'd floated almost to the surface, near enough to waking to be aware of the hard, masculine body she cuddled, aware of his scent and the even sound of his breathing, so that she carried both with her as she slipped back down in the trough of sleep.

So Sara was aware of Raz's nightmare almost as soon as he was.

When she emerged from a deeper doze this time she was already troubled, aware on some level that the body she sprawled across was no longer limp with sleep. Before she opened her eyes she knew Raz's breathing was ragged, his body tense. And while Sara had never in her life slept the night through with a man, she was accustomed to waking quickly and entirely, so her mind was working from the second she opened her eyes.

Which was just as well. Otherwise it would have come as quite a shock when he suddenly cried "No!" and threw her off of him.

It was still pretty startling.

She landed awkwardly on the very edge of the bed, started to slip, grabbed at the covers and ended up taking most of them with her as she slid to the floor. Her grip on the covers slowed her enough that she hit the floor quite gently. She sat there, blinking at the window. The light had a peculiar, misty quality, and where the curtains were cracked she saw only white on the other side of the glass.

Fog, she realized. A thick fog must have rolled in last night.

He muttered something and moved restlessly. Sara collected her wits enough to kneel there next to the bed and look at him. She could see the nightmare in his face—troubled, sweat-dampened. It hurt her heart to see him like this. She reached out, intending to take his arm, trying to wake him.

He said just one word, but he spoke clearly this time. It was a name. A woman's name.

Marguerite.

Raz came out of the nightmare all at once, panting and panicked. The blood—the blood—

He stared up at the ceiling, and slowly his fists unclenched. He was at the beach house. It was morning. And Sara...

Sara? He reached out but didn't find her. He turned his head and saw her. She was watching him solemnly, her chin resting on her forearm. "Sara?" He licked dry lips. "What are you doing on the floor?"

"Good question. You're a pretty restless sleeper, you know that?"

Horror filled him. He sat up. "I put you there? I didn't—hurt you?"

"Oh, no." She climbed back up in the bed. "Nothing like that. You were having a nightmare, though."

The nightmare. He'd pushed Marguerite away, as he did every time. And it had been too late, just like it was every time, every single damned time. He closed his eyes.

Sara's hand stroked his arm gently. He shuddered and pulled back. "For God's sake, don't touch me now." He could still feel the blood on him, warm and wet. He leaned his head forward in his hands. "Don't touch me."

Her voice was as soft as his was rough. "That must be a pretty heavy-duty nightmare."

He laughed once, without humor. "I told you. I'm a mess." The living warmth of Marguerite's blood had never been part of the nightmare before. Everything about the dream had always been cold, even the rich, red blood, as frozen as the snow that, in the dream, surrounded them both.

But not this time. This time Raz remembered clearly how warm her blood had felt when it splattered his face and chest.

Did that mean he was getting worse?

"It usually helps to talk," she said. "I know it isn't easy, but—"

"You don't know a damned thing." And she wouldn't. Ever. He wouldn't let Sara be touched by the ugliness that was part of him. He got out of bed, pulled open a drawer and grabbed his clothes. "I'm going for a run on the beach. You'll stay here this time, you hear me? No tagging after me." He fixed her with a look intended to intimidate.

He missed the mark slightly. Instead of intimidating her, he'd hurt her. She nodded once, the wince of rejection echoing in her sad eyes.

Ten

Sara sat on the couch, sipping her coffee with one hand and petting Mac with the other. The big cat still didn't like to stay inside for long, but she was making progress. He'd been out all night, but he'd been ready enough to come in for breakfast by the time she and Raz got up around nine. And now that he'd eaten he was willing to join her on the couch and let her practice her petting skills.

Only she kept forgetting what she was supposed to be doing. Her hand paused as she stared out the big double windows that faced the sea. Not that she could see much. Fog clung to land and sea alike, a thick, spectral blanket. But fog wasn't enough to keep Raz in. He was like Mac that way. Raz had gone on his run just as he always did, as if this morning were no different from any other.

Perhaps it wasn't, for him. Sara stared out the window at the ghostly insides of the cloud that had decided to sit on their island. She rubbed Mac's fur while she tried to think about something other than the man who had become her lover last night.

Her temporary lover.

It was a chilly day, brisk enough to give her wistful thoughts of a fireplace. Lacking that, she'd turned on the radio and plugged in the lights on her tree. Sara glanced over at the tree now, enjoying the every-colored lights, the carefully hung icicles and angels, bugles and beads. She smiled. Her Christmas tree gave her something of the same feeling she got when she jump-started a tired heart and it regained its rhythm. Or when someone came into the ER so bloodied and broken that each breath was a battle fought against all the odds—and then won that battle, over and over and over, and lived.

Miracles. She believed in them. Oh, they weren't available on demand, and they didn't always go to those who seemed the most deserving. They simply *were,* like rain and wind… and fog. Sara knew how it felt to break her heart fighting to find a miracle for a patient and losing the fight, because that extra breath of magic or fate wasn't hers to give.

But miracles did happen. Sometimes.

Music swelled in the background as the radio played "Deck the Halls." Sara thought about Christmas and Raz and her little tree—which still lacked something.

Presents.

Mac butted his head against her hand, reminding her of her duties. She chuckled. "I know what you want to find under that tree," she said, rubbing him along the jaw the way he liked. "Tuna fish. What do you think that big, two-legged alley cat might want?"

Sara wasn't at all sure what to get Raz, but she'd find something. Maybe she'd call Livvy and see if she wanted to go shopping later. Maybe…

No, she told herself firmly. She wasn't going to tell Raz about Harry's invitation—or summons—to ride one of his motorcycles. Nor would she go shopping with Livvy, or do anything else that encouraged others to see her and Raz as a couple. Because it would be too easy for her to start thinking of them as a couple, too. And what they shared was purely temporary.

She had to remember that. The last thing she wanted was to develop expectations. She wasn't going to make herself pathetic or Raz uncomfortable by making the kind of emotional demands her mother used to make of her father. It had never worked. Sara used to wonder why her mother couldn't see that she only drove her father farther away by insisting he give more than he was capable of giving.

Mac pushed his head against her hand, reminding her of her duties. "You don't mind making demands, do you, fella?" she said, smiling. "But I'll bet you aren't going to cry or throw things if I don't pet you."

She sipped her coffee, glad that she'd have something under the tree for herself soon. She'd seen to that this morning, when she called and checked her messages and learned that her aunt's package had finally arrived. She wasn't expecting any presents from Raz. He seemed almost angry about the holiday. No, she wouldn't count on getting anything from him.

She wondered if his attitude about Christmas had something to do with his demons. The ones he wouldn't tell her about.

Sara needed to help Raz as badly as she'd needed, all those years ago, to walk again. But how could she help him if he wouldn't talk to her? It was worse than trying to diagnose an unconscious patient, because with a patient she'd be able to order tests. With a patient she'd have some idea what to do. With Raz she just had questions.

Raz was still a cop. In the way his mind worked and in the loyalties that went heart deep, he was still part of the police force. So why had he taken leave?

What had happened to him between two and four months ago to put him in the hospital, leaving that scar on his thigh?

Who was Marguerite?

Sara sipped at her coffee and tried not to hurt herself, wondering about the woman who haunted his dreams. When the cellular phone rang, Mac was irritated because she stopped petting him and stood up to answer it, but Sara didn't mind the interruption. Not at all.

The fog was wet and chilly in his face and lungs. He couldn't see more than a few feet ahead of him as he ran, but he didn't let that slow him any.

Some changes happen more suddenly than others. When they'd first arrived at the island, Raz had gone to the beach to run because he wanted to get away. Now he ran because he needed it—needed the challenge, the strain, the sense that he was rebuilding something one breath at a time. He liked the slap of his feet on the hard-packed sand, the cries of the gulls and the endless sighing of the ocean. He accepted the loneliness.

He was winded when he dropped to a slow jog for the last half mile, his breathing harsh as he dragged in lungfuls of foggy, salty air. Not as winded as he had been a couple of days ago, though. Certainly not as winded as he would have been a couple of months ago, before he stopped smoking.

While he ran, he didn't think. Now that he'd slowed to a cool-down jog, however, the problems pressing on his mind returned.

Sara might have thought the question of who was to be her bodyguard was settled. Raz knew better. Oh, right now he was all she had, as either lover or protector, but he couldn't keep both roles. Though he hoped...

Ah, that was the surprise, wasn't it? Hope. He'd thought himself dead to that twisty beast. Yet here it was, subtle as a snake and twice as sneaky, coiled up tight in his gut, trying to taste tomorrow with its forked tongue. He didn't trust that feeling, no—but because of Sara he couldn't deny it. Raz hoped very much that once he gave up the role of bodyguard, he could remain Sara's lover. For a time.

He'd considered calling his brother while she was in the shower. He could have had Tom engage someone from North's agency and presented her with a fait accompli, but he'd decided to wait and confront her directly after marshaling all possible threats, pleas and arguments. Sara Grace was one stubborn woman. It wasn't going to be easy to head her in a direction she didn't want to go.

And yet, he thought as he slowed to a walk and moved to the dry, shifting sand between him and the house, Sara was a doctor. As such, she was susceptible to logic. He just had to make it clear to her why he couldn't be counted on to protect her now that they were lovers.

She's susceptible to something else, too, he thought. His body hardened as he thought of yet another way of swaying a stubborn mouse. Between sex and logic, he thought as he approached the back door, surely he could persuade Sara to be sensible.

He wasn't alarmed when he unlocked the door, opened it and saw that she was talking on the phone. Not until she turned and he saw her face.

He closed and locked the door. "What's wrong?"

"Your brother's on the phone." Her skin was as pale as her eyes were dark and unsettled. She held out the cellular phone. As soon as he took it, she walked over to the windows.

She wasn't using her cane today, he noticed. She also wasn't looking at him. Oddly reluctant, Raz put the receiver to his ear. "So what's up?"

Tom's voice said dryly, "First tell me if you're sleeping with her."

Raz called his brother a name that didn't flatter their mother.

"Because if your, uh, condition has improved and you *are* sleeping with her, you're in trouble. You didn't tell her about the drugs that have gone missing from Memorial, or how that affects her situation. Women don't like it when you hold out on them."

"It's a mistake to tell civilians any more than you have to." He watched Sara carefully not watching him. She stood very still, hugging her elbows close to her body and studying the view outside as if it were infinitely fascinating. Raz's eyes narrowed. He'd noticed that when she got mad she started hugging herself, as if she could physically hold her anger in.

"She's not Marguerite Ramirez, Raz."

Anger streaked, white-hot, down Raz's spine, stiffening it. "Damn right she's not."

"Then don't make her pay for—"

"Listen," Raz said, "if you have something to say about the case, get it said. Because you sure as hell aren't qualified to set up shop as my therapist. Did you decide to fill her in on everything I hadn't told her?"

There was a moment's silence. "I told her about the drug situation at Memorial, yes, and how that potentially endangers her."

Raz cursed, low voiced and foul, and started to pace.

"It seemed like a good idea after she asked me to pick up a box her landlord was holding for her. The one she called him about this morning."

He stopped dead. "She called Mathews? The chief of surgery at Memorial?" Fear crawled up the back of his throat, the taste of it rank and immediate.

"It's not as bad as it sounds. Mathews is on our list of suspects, yes, but well down that list for a number of reasons. She didn't tell him where she was, and she used the cellular phone, so the call won't show up on his caller ID. Assuming he has one."

Anger got his feet moving again. He headed for the far end of the room, away from Sara. "What the hell was she thinking of?"

"Christmas."

"I don't see what that—"

"Her aunt sends her a box with a couple of presents in it every year. She wanted it," Tom said.

Raz scowled, swallowed, and forced his voice to steady down. "So, you don't think her location has been compromised?"

"I don't see how. Even if Mathews is the guilty party, she didn't tell him her location, and she called him from an untraceable number."

Raz didn't respond immediately. He reached the far end of

the room, turned and stared at the small, still figure silhouetted against the windows that were white with fog. In the momentary silence the bright voices singing "Silver Bells" on the radio sounded obscenely cheery to him.

"All right," he said at last. "We'll stay here."

He asked Tom for an update on the investigation then, and tried to focus on the concrete puzzle pieces his brother had turned up instead of remembering the softness of Sara's face when she slept. Or her expression when she'd climaxed that first time, overtaken as much by astonishment as by passion. Or the way she'd looked and felt afterward, when she lay naked and happy and achingly vulnerable in his arms.

Sara isn't like Marguerite, he told himself desperately. But he was afraid that, in one important way, she was.

Though Sara wasn't looking at Raz, she knew it the moment he stopped pacing. She didn't turn, even when she heard him tell his brother goodbye and set down the phone. She cupped her elbows in her palms and told herself she was not going to make emotional demands of a man who was undoubtedly giving her all he could.

But she was so angry. And so hurt.

"All right," he said, coming toward her. He wore his ragged sweats again. His hair was wet from the fog, and clung damply to his forehead and neck. "It looks like no harm was done. But you have to promise me you won't do anything like this again."

"I wouldn't have done it this time," she said, biting off each word, "if you'd told me the truth about the situation."

His voice turned cool and civil. "Sleeping with me doesn't entitle you to confidential information on the progress of an investigation."

"But it's not *your* investigation, is it?" She turned, her hands dropping to make fists at her sides. "You're not a cop, remember? You may not have completely cut your ties with the force, but you're as much a civilian in this case as I am, so by what right did you withhold information from me?"

His eyes were flat and unrevealing. "Do you feel better now that you know?"

"That's not the point! I'm upset because you treated me like a child. Is that really what you think of me? That I can't handle the truth if it comes in an ugly package?"

"If you want me to apologize, you're out of luck." He shook his head. "Sara, when I came in just now, your face was white with shock because you'd just learned that someone you work with—your boss, maybe, or a friend—set you up to be killed. Life has been hard enough on you. I wanted to spare you that one particular pain."

Her shoulders stiffened. "Oh, I've run into that attitude before. I just didn't expect it from you. People often want to protect the poor little cripple, but slipping pity between two slices of compassion doesn't make it a more palatable meal."

He moved fast when he wanted to. So fast, and with such an alarming expression on his face, that she took an instinctive step back.

"Don't." He grabbed her shoulders. "Don't you ever accuse me of thinking of you that way. My God, do you know how much I admire you? Your courage humbles me. When I think of all you've done with your life—"

"Don't." Hot tears filled her eyes. She shoved hard at his hands, knocking them off her shoulders. "Don't put yourself down, and don't put me up on some—some pedestal. I'm like everyone else. I get scared and lonely and I do stupid things, selfish things sometimes. And I don't know what to say to people, how to make friends. I didn't even know how to p-pet a cat until Livvy showed me." She blinked furiously.

He smiled crookedly. "If you're trying to persuade me of your faults, you're doing a poor job of it. Even if I considered shyness a flaw, which I don't, I've seen you shed it as easily as you take off a coat when you step inside the emergency room."

"That's different." She shrugged. "When I've got a patient, I forget about myself. The rest of the time…maybe it's not a sin to be boring, but it's hardly a virtue."

"Not boring." He lifted his hands to her face. His fingers were firm along her jawbone. "Never that. With your clothes on, you're the most fascinating woman I know—strong and capable and funny. With them off..." His voice dropped, turning coaxing. "I like you best with your clothes off, pretty Sara."

She was silent, looking up at him through damp eyes. So many feelings were slipping through her, each calling for her to attend to it, to grasp and understand it. She had no idea what to say.

He shook his head slightly. "Have you noticed that the longer you hang around me, the better you get at being angry?"

That brought a hesitant smile to her face. "Practice makes perfect?"

"Maybe I am good for something, then. Aside from this." His fingers moved in a deliberate caress.

That was all it took. Her heart started drumming, sending a rhythmic message that was echoed in quick, excited pulses in other places on her body, places he'd touched and known last night. Places that wanted his touch again. Her lips parted. She put her hands on his chest.

He felt the same drumming. She knew he did, because she saw the taut look of his skin across his cheekbones. She felt the kick of his heart beneath her palms. Yet his eyes, his lovely chocolate-candy eyes, still looked so sad. And instead of kissing her he pulled her close, pressing her head against his chest, wrapping his arms around her. "Sara," he said, "will you be very honest with me?"

"That's really all I know how to be." Being held close like this, cuddled without kissing, was a remarkable feeling. She thought maybe she could stay just like this for the next year or two. "Either honest or quiet."

"What do you feel for me?"

After a moment she said, "Maybe I'd rather be quiet than honest this time."

She heard the ghost of a chuckle from him, felt his fingers

trace a shiver along the back of her neck. "I do care about you, Sara."

Now she wanted to pull away, almost as much as she'd wanted to linger in the circle of his arms a second ago. "But that's all you feel. Yes. I know that." *Temporary,* she reminded herself. That's what she was to him. She couldn't be angry about that, because it wasn't his fault.

He was silent for a long time, so long she thought he didn't mean to speak again at all. She pressed her head against his chest so she could hear, faintly, the measured beat of his heart, which blended right in with the *pa-rum-pa-pum-pum* refrain of the song playing on the radio.

His fingers sifted through the short fringe of her hair. "You're such a sensible woman. You have to know better than to get involved with someone like me."

She lifted her head. "You mean because I'm so dull and you're—"

"No, dammit, that's not what I mean!" He drew a deep breath. "Who do you see when you look at me, Sara? What do you see?"

"There are rather a lot of versions of you, aren't there?" she said thoughtfully. "I like all of them I've seen so far, but I'll admit I like some more than others."

He smiled ruefully. "So you see me as something of a split personality?"

"No." She reached up and ran her fingertips along his cheek. She loved the texture of his skin there, freshly shaved and so very male, and she loved having the freedom to touch him when she wanted. "No, you're just more changeable than most people. And you're used to acting a part, so you do tend to fall into your roles sometimes when you want to be alone and can't be."

"You're a little scary, you know that? Maybe...no," he said, shaking his head, "it doesn't matter. I still have to—you never did answer my question."

She'd hoped he'd forgotten his stupid question. "I don't want to."

"Maybe I'm wrong. I hope to hell I am, because I don't want you to...to make a mistake."

Well, she could reassure him on that. However it ended, what she felt wasn't wrong. "I'm not."

"Sara." He took a deep breath, let it out. "I have to say this flat-out. I don't want you to love me. The last woman who thought she did paid for her mistake with her life."

She winced. Obviously her feelings were no secret. Following fast on the heels of that first selfish hurt came the knowledge of *his* pain that had echoed in those quiet words, an echo that stole inside and hollowed her out.

Her arms tightened around him. "You blame yourself."

"Oh, yes. Because it was my fault. There's no doubt of that."

"Marguerite," she whispered.

He stiffened. "What? How did you—"

"Your dream. You said her name just before you woke up."

He said nothing, and his body refused the comfort she wanted to give, remaining stiff with either pain or rejection. She had no idea how to reach him, no womanly intuition to guide her.

Well, she thought, if instinct is silent, there's always logic. "Why is it your fault?"

"Why? Because I lied to her and used her."

Logic wasn't enough. It didn't tell her what to do with the emotions choking her—or the ones haunting him. "Who was she?"

"No one," he said softly, his eyes lost. "She was no one at all, really. Just one of a lot of damaged souls who grow up too fast and too hard on the streets. She was Jamie Jones's girlfriend. It was an identity of sorts—his money and his status in the 'hood, plus her beauty, made her stand out. That's what she needed, you see. To be real to other people so she would be real to herself. Jamie was scum and he treated her badly, but he was mid-level scum. Just the sort I needed," he finished bitterly, "to lead me to the upper-level scum."

"You used her to get to him?" Yet he'd cared about her. She could see that in the bleakness of his eyes, sense it in the tension of his body.

"You catch on quickly, don't you? She said once that no one had ever really listened to her. I listened, all right. I wanted to hear all about Jones's plans."

Sara had developed a matter-of-fact manner for speaking to badly traumatized patients. She used it now. "You were operating undercover. You couldn't very well tell her the truth."

"Oh, I tried that, too, later on. I'm nothing if not inconsistent. The department says that's where I went over the line—that and the fact that I took her to bed. Your face tells me you agree that going to bed with her was not admirable behavior. Let me reassure you that the rest of it, the lying and using, was well within the regs for undercover work. Not that I got in serious trouble. My supervisor entered a reprimand in my record, gave me a talking to, and that's as far as it went."

Abruptly he dropped his arms and moved away, putting his back to her. "Marguerite *died,* and I got a lecture."

"Raz—"

"You're going to have to hire someone else, Sara."

Her breath stopped in her throat. *Not yet.* It couldn't be over yet. Her hand flew to her chest. She was surprised to feel her heart still beating there, sturdy and strong. She took a step forward. "I don't want anyone else."

"I can't do this. I can't be responsible for your life when—I would have told Tom to get someone from North's agency while I had him on the phone, but I thought I owed it to you to discuss it with you first." He started moving again, heading restlessly for the far wall where the windows were whited out by fog.

"Is this supposed to be a discussion, then? It sounded more like an ultimatum."

He turned, his eyes hooded and distant. "I can't be both your bodyguard and your lover."

She took a deep, shuddery breath of relief. "Do I get to choose which one I want you to be?"

"Yes."

"I think you know my choice already. I think you know exactly how I feel." Her feet took another step toward him and another. "Though we've both been careful not to say it straight-out. But you have to tell me what you want, too."

"I want to be your lover," he said softly. "And that's damnably unfair to you, but—"

"Shut up, Raz." She drew closer.

His eyebrows went up. "Shut up?"

Sara stopped about ten feet away, unable to make herself go the last few feet when his expression was still so closed. "I don't like it when you keep telling me, in various ways, that I can't be trusted to make my own decisions."

"I don't want to hurt you."

She shrugged. "Life hurts sometimes." Sara had spent too long in therapy to think of pain as something to be avoided at all costs. She respected it, listened to the warning it gave, but she didn't let it control her life. "Promise me one thing."

"If I can."

"Don't choose for me. Let me decide for myself what I can and can't handle."

He studied her face for a long moment before, reluctantly, the corners of his mouth tilted up wryly. "If you're asking me to be selfish instead of noble, I think I can manage that."

"Good." She nodded and cleared her throat. "That's good. So, what am I supposed to do with a second bodyguard?"

"None of the things you'll be doing with me, I trust. I'll see if North can get someone here by tonight, tomorrow morning at the latest."

Then the two of them would still be here. Together. She nodded slowly. "All right. I'm really not very good at compromise, you know."

His eyes were soft and sad. "You told me that once."

Mac's sudden, loud complaint startled them both. Sara looked behind her. The big cat sat near the front door, looking cross. "I think he wants out."

She turned, glad for the reprieve. She felt swamped and inadequate, unable to help either of them.

Raz's voice stopped her as she reached for the doorknob. "Open it just enough for him to go out, and don't stand in the doorway when you do."

Sara felt foolish, hiding behind the door to let her cat out when Javiero was so far away. But Raz sounded grim and certain, so she did as she was told. The second the door opened, Mac transformed himself into an orange streak bolting for freedom. She sighed, watching him race across the porch and jump down. "I keep hoping he won't feel such a strong need to escape every time the door opens."

"He may never change, you know. He was on the streets for a long time. Some of those lessons are hard to unlearn."

How long, she wondered, had Raz been on the streets?

Just as she was closing the door, she heard a newly familiar roar approaching. She paused. Dimly, through a thin spot in the fog, she glimpsed Harry on his motorcycle. Livvy rode behind him, hugging her short, merry husband tight as the two of them appeared, ghostly shapes in the enveloping fog, and then vanished. The sound of the engine faded slowly.

Longing rose up in Sara, clear as rain and twice as sad. She wanted, oh, how she did want, what Livvy and Harry had.

She took a deep breath, then closed the door and turned. Raz had crossed the room to stand behind her, only a step away. "What did you have in mind for us to do today?" she asked.

He didn't reach for her, but his eyes lost some of their bleak distance when they focused on her. "Whatever you like. What would you like to do today, pretty Sara?"

She ran a nervous tongue over her lips. Risk had a lemony taste, tart and exciting. "I think I could use some therapy."

He frowned. "You said I didn't hurt you last night. Are you sore? What's wrong?"

"That's not what I mean." She managed to take that last step, to close the distance between them and put her hands on his chest. She smiled up at him, her cheeks heating slightly.

"I'm not sore at all. Um...maybe I should have said I need a workout."

"Oh, I see. A workout." His smile spread slowly. When he put his hands at her waist, his wicked thumbs easily wandered up her sides to tickle the undersides of her breasts. "Good idea. I think we could, ah, work something out, between the two of us."

The tingles, the thrill, the heat were already becoming familiar. She intended to follow that heat wherever it led her, however temporary the trail might be. In just a minute. "There's one other thing I want to do today."

He bent to nibble on her neck. "What's that?"

"I want you to take me for a ride on one of Harry's motorcycles."

Eleven

"I can use all the help I can get," Livvy said cheerfully. "I'm warning you, though, the kitchen is a disaster."

"I love to bake." Sara waited while her hostess pushed the button that closed the garage door. It was three o'clock. Raz had just left with Harry on some mysterious errand that she hoped, in spite of her determination not to expect anything, might be Christmas shopping. Why else would he have looked so consciously secretive? Why else would he have smiled at her in such a way when he asked her to stay with Livvy?

Livvy led her through the door into the main house. "So did you enjoy your ride?"

"The fog made it kind of spooky, but in a nice way." Although the cloudy blanket had thinned by afternoon, it never had lifted completely. The air remained damp and still.

Their route to the kitchen, Sara was glad to see, took them down a different hallway, not the one where she'd seen the barracuda clinging to Raz last night. "It's funny," she said.

"I never would have thought I'd like riding motorcycles, but I do."

"Harry's contagious."

Oh, I hope so, Sara thought. Raz needed a dose of Harry's cheerful self-confidence. "I think he's wonderful. In a bossy sort of a way."

Livvy chuckled. "I can't argue with that. Here we are," she said, pushing open a swinging door. "Remember that I warned you."

Livvy had told Sara she'd decided to try her hand at Christmas baking this year, but had made a mess of things. Sara, of course, had offered to help, but until she stood in the large, modern kitchen, now smelling strongly of burned cookies, vanilla and spices, she hadn't quite understood the magnitude of the mess Livvy was capable of.

The sink overflowed with dirty pans and baking sheets. A food processor and its attachments, all covered in some sticky dough, occupied one counter. The work island in the center of the kitchen held flour and sugar, boxes and tins and bottles of all sorts, dirty bowls and spoons and measuring cups. Oranges had spilled out of one sack onto the floor. The top of the stove and part of the floor were dusted with powdered sugar.

And there were cookies everywhere. Burned cookies. Odd, messy glops of cookies. Underbaked crumbs of cookies. Lots and lots and lots of cookies.

"You've never done this before, have you?" Sara asked.

"I like to try new things," Livvy said cheerfully. "I've got plenty of flour and other stuff, but we may need to buy more cookie sheets. What do you think?"

"I think," Sara said, unbuttoning her sleeves so she could roll them up, "we had better get to work." She looked down at her hands. The lying gold ring still gleamed there, and she decided she'd had enough of that. She pulled it off and put it in her pocket. When she did, her hand encountered another metal shape. "Here's your key back, Livvy."

"Oh, you keep it. You should have a key to your honeymoon cottage."

She sighed. "Before we start, there's something I need to tell you."

"What do you think?" Raz said, holding up a tiny little top that was rigid with sequins. He needed to find Sara the right thing to wear, something that made her feel daring and special, for his surprise to work.

But not too daring, or he'd never get her to try it on.

"I think it's a good thing you brought me along," Harry said. "You weren't joking when you said you had bad taste, were you?"

"Unusual taste," Raz corrected him. "Not bad, just unusual." He studied the little top he held. So maybe the swirls of yellow and green and purple sequins were a bit outrageous. He liked it. He had to admit, though, he would probably have trouble getting Sara into it. Reluctantly he hung it back on the rack. "You have any suggestions?"

"Here," Harry said, holding out a silk shirt with narrow red and green stripes.

Raz eyed it. "Too ordinary."

"Your Sara doesn't like to call attention to herself."

"I know, but...it just needs to be right. Something different, but not too different. Something she can wear to Fat Fannie's."

Harry's eyebrows went up. "That's where you want to take her? No, no, that's not Sara's sort of place. Take her someplace nice."

"She doesn't want someplace nice. That's the point. She's never been to a real, boot-stomping honky-tonk."

When Sara had told him that earlier, she'd sounded so wistful he had immediately decided to surprise her by taking her to a honky-tonk tonight. After their ride, Raz had asked Harry where to find something dressy for Sara, and this was where they'd ended up—Friday Nights, a small, rather expensive women's clothing shop in Corpus Christi. They were the only men in the place, a fact that the red-haired clerk seemed to find suspicious.

"Do you think it's just us?" Raz said the third time the clerk glanced warily over at them while waiting on other customers. "Or do you think she doesn't approve of male customers?"

Harry shrugged. "She is not the woman who waited on me before, so I don't know. And in truth, we don't look very respectable, my friend—me still in my leathers from my ride earlier, and you in that, ah, *colorful* T-shirt."

Raz had dealt with too many people whose bankrolls were a great deal healthier than their souls, to have much patience with those who confused appearances with real decency. He ignored the snobbish clerk and pulled out a green satin shirt with ties at the waist. "What do you think? She can wear her jeans with it."

"I think," Harry said, "that shirt has no buttons. And while I would not mind seeing Sara in a shirt with no buttons, I don't believe she—"

"Never mind." Raz shoved it back on the rack.

Harry moved over to the next rack. "So," he said, "you will take her new bodyguard with you on this date to Fat Fannie's?"

Raz frowned at the dozens of shirts in front of him. "North's man won't get here until tomorrow." He'd told Harry about the expected arrival of Sara's new bodyguard on the way here, adding that Harry could go ahead and tell Livvy the truth when he got home. After tomorrow, it would be obvious he and Sara weren't honeymooners.

"How strange," Harry said, pulling a shirt from the rack. "Her danger must be great if she needs two men guarding her, yet you are taking her out tonight. This is safe for her?"

"She'll still just have one bodyguard when North's man arrives."

"Ah. I see. What do you think of this top? Very sexy, yes, with the lace?"

Raz frowned. "It's black." He couldn't picture Sara in such a sophisticated color. "She bakes bread, you know."

"Does she? Women feel sexy in black," Harry said. "But if you do not like it…"

"I don't." He pulled out a stretchy knit shirt in bright orange. A stylized sun in glittery gold sent short, shiny rays out from its middle. "What do you think of this?"

"I think it would suit my Livvy very well, but not your Sara. Now, let me see if I understand. Today, when you still pretend to be her husband, you are also her bodyguard, but not tomorrow when the other bodyguard arrives. Then you will be her lover, but not her husband."

Raz's jaw clenched. "If you have something to say, just say it."

"No, no, I talk too much, that's all. Only I wonder…what do you think of this blue one? No? Well, I do wonder why you pretended to be her husband at all. Such an odd thing to do."

"Most people will leave a honeymooning couple alone," Raz said dryly. "I had hoped to stay isolated while we were on the island."

"Livvy changed your plans, did she?" He chuckled. "But that doesn't explain why you claimed to be married. People would have granted privacy to a young bachelor who brought a pretty woman to his beach house for a few days, and for the same reason. They would assume you and she had other things to do than socialize."

"Sara isn't the sort of woman you—" Raz heard what he was saying and grimaced. "Look, it's obvious you know that the relationship between Sara and me is no longer professional. That's why someone else has to be her bodyguard. But I'm damned if I know what your point is."

"My point is that your relationship with her has never been professional, however much you may have persuaded yourself this was so. Not in her mind. Not in yours. Now that," he said, turning to admire the blouse in Raz's hands, "is more the sort of thing you want for Sara."

"It's pretty." He looked at the simple white silk blouse with a row of tiny rhinestone buttons down the front. "But I don't think it's right for Fat Fannie's."

"Find another one for the honky-tonk, and buy that one for her for Christmas."

"No." Raz hung the blouse up again. "Not for Christmas."

"And why is that? You have already bought her a present?"

"Leave it alone, Harry." Raz moved away slightly.

Harry followed. "I'll tell you what I think."

The red-haired lady rang up her last customer's purchase and glanced over at them again.

"You won't be here on Christmas, will you?" Harry said, stopping to look Raz in the eye. "That's why you must give her presents and take her out tonight. Because after this, you will leave."

Raz would have told him the truth then—if he'd known what it was. But what could he say? Did he tell Harry that he wanted to stay with Sara forever, or that he wanted to leave her? Both were true, or maybe neither. She made him feel too much. The snow was melting, the frozen place inside him giving way to her warmth, and he wanted desperately to be gone—just as desperately as he wanted to bind her to him. If only he could be sure he wasn't using her....

What was he going to do? He had no idea.

It was a relief when the red-haired lady hurried up, smiling like a toothpaste ad. "Perhaps you gentlemen could use a little help deciding?"

"No," Raz said. For some reason he reached for the top Harry had suggested, the black, lacy one that was surely wrong for a gentle soul like Sara. "I'll take this one."

Sara stared in the mirror, fascinated. The woman who looked back was a stranger with eyes darkened into mystery by the liner and mascara Livvy had insisted she borrow. Her hair—well, not too much could be done with hair as short as hers, but she'd washed it and fluffed it.

And her lips were red. Not the pale pink Sara wore when-

ever she bothered with lipstick, but a bright, hot, siren red—
one of Raz's gifts. As for her clothes...

She smoothed the lacy sleeve of the stunning little black
top Raz had given her. She'd been so surprised after he and
Harry returned and Raz had handed her the shopping bag,
telling her he hoped she would wear the contents out on a date
with him that night.

Maybe surprise hadn't been her first reaction, she admitted
as she stretched her arms behind her to fasten the tiny hook
and eye. Maybe, just for a second, she'd been disappointed.
Even though she had told herself not to expect Christmas from
Raz, she'd hoped...but when she saw his gift, surprise and
pleasure had washed away whatever else she'd felt.

The bodice was a stretchy knit with a daring sweetheart
neckline, the knit topped with black lace. The sleeves were
lace, too, a stretchy lace as black as midnight. Her skin looked
so pale next to all that black.

Did he truly see her like this? Like a woman who could
wear black lace next to her skin?

Sara took a deep breath. She was ready. As ready, at least,
as she ever would be. Now she had to walk out there and see
if he still thought she was a black-lace woman when he saw
her wearing his gift.

Raz paced the big room, unable to sit still. All the quiet
was making him nervous. He'd turned the radio off when Sara
went to get ready because the stations were all playing Christmas music now, but the silence grated on him almost as badly
as "Jingle Bells" had.

He wore a sports jacket with his T-shirt, jeans and boots.
He was too warm and too dressed-up for Fat Fannie's, but he
didn't have much choice. Sara might dislike his shoulder harness and the gun it held, but he couldn't take her out without
it.

He paused by the big windows to check the locks. Fog had
rolled in once more with the sunset, thicker than ever, so that
all the glass gave back was his own reflection and a ghostly

sketch of his surroundings, lit by the single lamp he'd left on. How much of a fool was he, he wondered, to take her out like this? Oh, he didn't expect to run into Javiero at Fat Fannie's, despite his determination to keep his gun with him. No, his folly lay in wanting to believe in the future he'd seen shining in Sara's eyes.

He was a mess. He'd told her that, but she was hoping for a future together, anyway. He'd seen that hope in her eyes, so what did he do? He bought her presents and took her out. It wasn't right. Lord, he thought, running his hand over the top of his head, he didn't even know how much of his plans for tonight were for her sake and how much were for his own. Her needs and his were all jumbled up in his mind.

Still, he could live with being a fool. He wasn't sure he could live with hurting Sara. He pulled the blinds closed and turned away from the windows. After tonight he would step back, give them both time to sort out what they felt.

What was taking her so long? Maybe she hated the top he'd bought and didn't know how to tell him. Sure, she'd *looked* pleased when she'd opened the bag and seen what he'd bought her, but Sara was too kind to insult someone's gift. Probably she hated it. Probably she thought he was trying to turn her into something she wasn't. Why had he bought her the black one, anyway? She wasn't—

The bedroom door opened. He turned.

She hovered uncertainly near the doorway. "It fits pretty well," she said, and smiled.

A smile like that on lips one whit less red might have looked shy. A glow like that in eyes any less artfully sultry than hers were tonight might easily be mistaken for innocence. And on a body less pale and perfect, that black lace might not have taken his breath away. For a long moment he couldn't speak.

"You don't like it," she said, her face falling.

"Not like it?" He shook his head and started for her. "I *like* a cold beer after mowing the lawn. I *like* hot peppers on my nachos. What that outfit does for me is on a whole other level from 'liking.'"

"Oh." She blinked once, self-conscious and happy. "Then you do think I look okay?"

"Not okay." He stopped in front of her and pulled her up against him. She felt even better than she looked. "Gorgeous. Ravishing. Good enough to eat." His smile was as wicked as the finger he used to draw a line from her collarbone down to her waist, her belly button, her… "If I hadn't already promised you dinner," he said, his finger hesitating just above the scandal zone, "I'd show you what I mean."

Her smile slipped. "If you'd rather not eat out—"

"Sara. Don't you know better than to let a man get away with promising you a night on the town and then reneging?"

"Well, no, I don't think I do. I haven't dated much," she confessed, "and I don't like to be demanding."

That, he suspected, was her mother's legacy. "Then I think we should get something straight. When I tell you I'm going to do something, you have every right to pitch a fit if I don't do it. Don't look so dubious. You're already getting better at being mad. If I continue to behave badly, we'll have you pitching some fine fits in no time." He gave her a quick, hard kiss on the lips. "We'd better go before all my worst instincts overwhelm me."

She started for the door beside him, then paused, looking at the table. A slightly limp poinsettia bloomed in a foil-wrapped pot tied with a big red bow. "Why—that's new. Did you buy it?" Her eyes were wide with surprise.

"It's nothing." He shrugged, uncomfortable. "Just an impulse. We stopped at the grocery store on the way home—Harry said Livvy needed a couple things—and they had dozens of them for sale. You seem to like having a lot of Christmas stuff around, so I thought…"

"Thank you," she said softly, and stretched up to kiss his cheek. "For everything."

He stood still for a moment, paralyzed by a simple kiss on the cheek and an absurd upwelling of pride. She'd liked his gifts, the black top and the poinsettia. He'd gotten that much right. He wanted, badly, to make the entire evening right for her. If he could do that much, maybe, just maybe, he could hope to be enough for her. Maybe he could find the courage to listen to the possibilities whispering in his ear.

Raz was smiling as he got Tom's canvas jacket and held it out for her.

She shook her head. "Not with this outfit."

He kicked himself for not thinking of getting her another, dressier jacket. "We'll take it with us, then." He carried the jacket over one arm, and crooked his other in an exaggeratedly formal way.

She smiled and took his arm. "So where are we going?"

"To the nearest steakhouse. After that—who knows?" He hadn't mentioned Fat Fannie's yet. He meant to surprise her.

"I've been eating too much beef."

"You can load up at the salad bar, then. Sorry, but I have to be firm on this point. You wouldn't realize this, being a transplanted Yankee and all, but steak is the traditional Texas meal for a first date." When they reached the front door he took a last look around the house, running over a mental checklist of locks and other precautions.

Mac grumbled near their feet.

"Uh-oh." She bent and pushed the cat away from the door. "I think we'd better leave him in. The radio mentioned that a storm front is on its way. I'd hate it if bad weather blows in and we aren't around to let him in."

"Okay, but this isn't going to be easy."

It wasn't. Raz was laughing by the time they made it onto the porch, after several failed attempts, without the cat. They could hear Mac inside, wailing his displeasure with them both.

Sara frowned. "Do you think he's going to be terribly unhappy in there?"

"He's mad, Sara, not miserable. He might sulk a bit, but it won't hurt him to stay in."

Sara had no memory, later, of what she ate for supper that night. She remembered instead the stories he told her about some of the visits he and his family had made to the island—

how they'd first met Livvy, and why his mother decided they needed a "family mailbox" to keep track of everybody, and made his father put a big, smooth rock by the front door. At first they'd all written their messages on the rock itself: "gone for groceries" or "back before ten" or "I love you, sweetheart"; eventually they ran out of room to write, and used it to hold notes to each other.

She remembered his laughter when she told him how she got the bird she'd named Mr. Greenjeans, and the way he held her hand as they left the restaurant. And she remembered the heat in his eyes.

Sara had no idea where they were when he pulled into the parking lot of a dingy-looking nightspot. It was apparently a popular place, in spite of its unprepossessing exterior. The lot was so crowded he had to squeeze the car into a barely-there spot between two pickups. Sara looked at the square, shabby building, then at the neon sign that advertised beer and dancing below the red glow of "Fat Fannie's."

Her heart sank. She didn't know how to dance. She was going to disappoint him. "Is this your surprise?"

"We don't have to stay here if you don't want to. I just thought you might like to see a real honky-tonk. You said..." His voice trailed off and he ran a hand over the top of his head, messing his shaggy hair even more. "Hell. This was one of my dumber ideas, wasn't it?" He reached out to restart the car.

This was another gift, she realized. Like the poinsettia and the top. He'd wanted to give her something new, something she'd never had before. Warmth burst inside her so quickly she didn't stop to think. She leaned over and kissed him. "This is wonderful. You're wonderful."

When she would have pulled back, he threaded his fingers through her short hair, cupping her head to change the angle, and kissed her back. Long and deliciously. When their mouths parted, his breathing sounded as disrupted as hers.

He asked her if she was ready to go home yet.

She laughed. "No, you promised me a honky-tonk."

He grinned and opened his door. "You're learning. Now, we don't have to dance," he said. Her side of the car was so close to one of the trucks she had to slide out on his side. "But you've been moving pretty easily today, so I figure your hip is up to a little slow dancing."

"Well," she said, fiddling with her hair, "my hip may be, but I'm not. The truth is, I never learned how to dance."

"No problem. You only have to know one dance to fit right in—the two-step. You can do it fast, slow, fancy or plain. It's simple enough for a cowboy with two left feet to learn when he has a little too much beer beneath his belt, so you won't have any trouble catching on."

She smiled, but she had no intention of making a fool of herself out on that dance floor.

Sara loved dancing.

Raz had been pretty sure she would, but he hadn't realized her eyes would turn into stars shining just for him by their second slow dance. He hadn't known how much he'd needed her to look at him that way.

It wasn't really him that put that light in her eyes, he told himself. Sara was hungry for romance, that was all. She'd needed a man to take the time to give her flowers and dancing...even if those flowers were a pot of slightly wilted poinsettias, and the dancing was done to a jukebox beneath a neon moon.

Even if that man was him.

She didn't love him. Not really. She was vulnerable, though, to the music on the jukebox, to the touch of romance he'd tried to give her—and to the silent music their bodies made as they moved together in the peculiar privacy of a dark, crowded dance floor. He danced her around in slow, small circles, putting no strain on her hip or leg, letting no distance come between them. Sara's body followed his effortlessly, as if she'd been dancing for years.

From the speakers at each end of the dance floor, Garth Brooks sang about cowboys and angels. She shifted herself a tiny bit closer to him. His heart stumbled and fell that last, tiny step.

Oh, God, he wanted her to love him.

Raz quit pretending he was dancing, wrapped his arms around her and laid his cheek against her hair. He stood there swaying with Sara in his arms.

When the song changed suddenly from the slow, dreamy "Cowboys and Angels" to the quick beat of "Midnight Cinderella," they both jumped. But they didn't let go of each other.

Raz grinned down at her. "Think it's midnight yet?"

"I'm not sure," she said, those stars shining brightly in her eyes. "But I think it's time to go home." And she gave a provocative little wiggle that sent his blood pressure soaring.

A slowly stirring wind had thinned the fog by the time they left the honky-tonk. Raz had his arm around Sara, who was pressed up against his side. He felt her shiver. The temperature had dropped while they were inside, making him think the weatherman had been right about the storm headed their way.

Raz insisted she put on his brother's canvas jacket when they got in the car. Only tatters of fog remained as the storm front moved in, but he drove slowly, anyway. He didn't want to rush a moment of their night together. They talked a little, but neither of them paid much attention to what was said. Both were intent on the gathering hum of desire, the anticipation of other slow, unhurried things they might do together when they got home.

Home. The beach house wasn't that, of course, and yet pulling up in the driveway with Sara at his side felt very much like coming home. He shut off the ignition, leaned over and found her mouth with his, giving both of them a taste of heat. "Let's go inside."

Her fingers stroking his cheek were more confident than her voice was. "We could wait a minute to go in. I haven't necked in the front seat of a car since I started high school."

Not since before the accident, in other words. Her hesitant

request slid into him as neatly as a scalpel parting healthy tissue, slipping deep inside to the part of him that had been frozen for so long. He wasn't cold there anymore. It hurt. "Another time, sweetheart. The temperature's dropping, and I don't want you getting goose bumps." Most of all he didn't want to be wearing his shoulder holster when he really kissed her.

He stepped out of the car. The wind off the ocean was sharp as a slap, scented with the ozone bite of the approaching storm. It was after midnight and very dark. None of the neighboring houses were still lit, except for the red and green lights that winked gaily along the rooftop of the house across the street.

But Raz had, of course, left the porch light on, so he saw the upended basket near the front door as soon as he rounded the hood of the car. "What in the world—?"

"Cookies, I think," Sara said wryly. She mounted the steps beside him, shaking her head as she looked over the damage. The basket had been sealed in colored cellophane and tied with a big bow, but the cellophane was torn, the basket tipped, and broken bits of cookies were scattered across the porch. "Look, there's a note under your mother's 'mailbox.' I'll bet it's from Livvy. She must have brought us some of those endless batches she and I baked this afternoon," she said, kneeling to get the note out from under the big rock.

He frowned as he put the key in the lock. "The wind didn't tip that basket over."

"Oh, I imagine some animal got into it. The leash laws don't seem to be strictly enforced here."

The lock clicked. Something about those scattered cookies bothered him. He turned the doorknob, trying to figure out—

"Mac!" Sara exclaimed from behind him. "Did you do this, you rotten cat? How did you get out? I—"

In one smooth, desperate motion Raz turned and launched himself at Sara. He hit her kneeling figure just as the door swung open. The two of them tumbled off the porch a split second before the terrible thunder of gunfire split the night.

Raz landed badly, with too much of his weight on Sara, but

he couldn't stop to see if she was all right. He rolled the two of them up against the concrete bunker formed by the raised porch as bullets whined overhead. He had his gun out before they finished moving.

The hail of bullets stopped. In the sudden silence, Raz knew Javiero was coming, knew that in another couple of seconds the punk would be standing over them with that damned Uzi. He got his feet under him and prayed he'd get off one good shot. Just one.

He heard two things as he pushed to his feet—an inhuman shriek loud enough to wake the dead, and Javiero's shrilly screamed obscenity. Then Raz was standing, gun extended, aiming for the chest of the little bastard whose weapon swung around wildly.

An enormous orange cat clung, tooth and claw, to Javiero's thigh.

"Police!" Raz shouted. "Drop it!"

But the scrawny youth didn't drop his Uzi. He swiped at Mac with it, snarling as he knocked the cat off and brought the barrel back up—towards Raz.

Raz squeezed the trigger.

Twelve

The blast from Raz's gun hurt Sara's ears, joining the terrifying echo of the Uzi's fusillade. She was bent over in a huddled heap, half-deafened and wholly immobilized by the death that had thundered overhead only seconds ago. She grabbed at Raz's leg, wanting to pull him down with her, out of the line of fire.

He vaulted up onto the porch.

She opened her mouth to call him back, and the breath she'd been holding shuddered out. It was silent. Silent. No one was shooting. She shivered once, gripped the edge of the porch and used it to get to her feet. She hurt in half a dozen places. Her weak leg didn't want to hold her up. She ignored those things.

Raz knelt next to Javiero's body, his fingers on the carotid artery in the throat.

She found her voice. "Is he dead?"

"Not yet. Are you all right?"

"Yes." Except that she had to move. If Javiero wasn't dead

yet, she had to try and keep him alive. The response was ingrained, automatic. Limping heavily, she started up the stairs, struggling to slide into her professional persona. He was a patient now, she told herself as she climbed that last step. A John Doe with a bullet wound. That's how she had to think of him.

She reached the Uzi first. Raz had moved it out of reach of the gang leader's outflung hand. The hole in his chest hadn't bled much. Bullet entry wounds seldom did. His head lay at an awkward angle next to the large, smooth stone where Livvy had left her note. His eyes were rolled back in his head, leaving slits with only the white showing.

There was blood on Raz's hand, too—the one he had used to test Javiero's pulse. His face was entirely blank when he looked up.

"You're all right?" she said. "He didn't hit you?"

"I'm not hit." He stood. The gun was still in his hand.

"Good. That's good." She took a deep breath and let it out slowly, trying to master the shakes. "Call it in. I have to start treatment."

He nodded once and went inside.

The aftermath of violence, as much as the adrenaline still trapped in her body, made her nauseous. She limped heavily as she took the last few steps to her patient. Oh, yes, definitely he was a patient, not a corpse, she saw. Corpses might have an ashy complexion, but they didn't sweat. His eyelids twitched. She lowered herself painfully to kneel beside him.

Remember the ABCs, she told herself, repeating the mantra of emergency personnel. Airway, Breathing, Circulation… "Are you conscious?" she said sharply as she gripped his chin in one hand. "Do you hear me? I have to check your airway."

His lids fluttered, but didn't open. She hesitated only a moment, thinking of the gloves she didn't have. Quickly she visually inspected her hands and found no cuts, then she checked inside his mouth to make sure his tongue hadn't fallen back in his throat.

No visible obstructions. Pulse rapid and shallow. Respiration shallow, too.

Raz's voice came from the open door. "An ambulance is on the way."

She didn't look up. "Good. What did you shoot him with?" The bullet had entered on the lower right portion of the chest, just above the lumbar region, it looked like, and traveled upward.

"A 9 mil."

"Hollow-point?" The patient stirred slightly. He seemed distressed, but not truly responsive.

"No."

Good. A hollow-point or dum-dum did its worst damage after entering the body, spreading out in a widening cone of destruction. A regular 9 mm bullet would punch straight through. She tucked fingers from both hands in the hole in the shirt and pulled, ripping it wider so she could see the wound better.

"Sara—"

"Not now." She waited, and a second later saw what she'd feared. Sure enough, the blood around the wound bubbled during inspiration. At least it was bright pink, rather than the deep red that would have indicated arterial blood.

She straightened and sighed, wanting her stethoscope. "He's got an open pneumothorax—a sucking chest wound. That's a hole in the chest wall right through to the lung, which is probably partially collapsed. Blood will drain into the chest cavity, which puts pressure on the heart. They'll take care of that in the ER. Right now—" She looked up. "Do you have a pocket knife?"

He nodded.

"Good. Give it to me, then get the plastic wrap from the kitchen and the petroleum jelly from the bathroom. And some towels. And hurry."

She used the knife to cut away the T-shirt, talking to the patient the whole time, telling him what she was doing. Though he remained nonresponsive, she knew he might come around at any time. Raz returned quickly with the supplies, and one corner of her mind noted his grim expression.

She understood, or thought she did. He'd shot a man—that man might die. No matter what the circumstances, that would eat at him.

As Sara blotted up the blood around the wound and smeared Vaseline around the bullet's entry hole, she realized she did have a compelling reason outside of her professional ethics to fight for this patient's life, after all. She didn't want Raz haunted by any more ghosts.

Raz handed her a square of plastic wrap. "I think Mac's okay. When Javiero knocked him loose, he took off running."

She looked up. "What? What did he do to Mac?"

"Your cat had his claws sunk in the bastard's leg. It kept Javiero too busy to shoot me." Raz grinned suddenly. "I owe that mutant monster a very big bowl of tuna fish."

She looked back at her patient. Tears stung her eyes. She blinked fiercely to clear her vision as she pressed the plastic over the wound.

"Hey, your cat is okay. He couldn't have run that fast if he'd been hurt."

"I didn't know about Mac. I didn't see him. I was hiding, all bent over—"

"He's okay." Raz said. "I'm sure of it."

"He attacked Javiero. He saved you." Emotion threatened to choke her. She had to take a deep, cleansing breath before she could resume her examination.

"I imagine he attacked on his own behalf," Raz said, "not mine. Javiero probably stepped on his tail."

She shook her head, unable to speak.

The patrol car arrived first, siren and lights blaring. Raz left her and went to deal with his fellow officers. He must have persuaded them to leave her alone, because no one bothered her while she completed her crude examination. The bullet had exited directly above the third right thoracic rib. She found a slight swelling at the back of his head and several lacerations in his right upper thigh, a couple of them deep enough that they still bled sluggishly.

Mac. He'd done that. Now he was missing.

The throb of a second siren cut through her worried thoughts just as the first fat raindrops fell. Sara forced her attention back to her patient, who was showing signs of returning to consciousness. A few minutes later the ambulance pulled up, its familiar cherry light strobing the night.

They managed to get their patient loaded before the rain cut loose completely.

The storm blew in fast and hard but was already over by the time Livvy drove Sara back to the beach house. Sara had stayed at the hospital for hours, first to give her statement to the officer who followed them in, then because she wanted to hear the results of Javiero's surgery. His condition had been downgraded from critical to serious when she left, which was pretty encouraging. That much good news she could give Raz.

Once she found him.

Livvy had joined her at the hospital about forty minutes after she got there. Raz had called and asked her to take Sara her cane and his brother's jacket. But Raz hadn't come himself. Nor was he at the beach house. Sara had called there several times, but no one had answered. She knew he hadn't been arrested or gone down to the police station for questioning or anything like that. The officer who took her statement had assured her of that much. So where was he?

She had no idea. Her mind came up empty every time she turned it to that question.

When they pulled up in front of the cottage, Sara thanked Livvy, told her to go home and got out of the car. Livvy ignored her and got out, too. "I'm not a bit tired," she announced. "And I'm not about to let you walk into that place alone, after everything that's happened."

If Livvy wondered why Sara was alone at such a time, she was kind enough not to say so.

Sara moved slowly. Her hip hurt, and she had a couple of

bruises from getting tackled and knocked off the porch, but those aches hardly mattered. No, the ache that troubled her was her certainty that something was wrong. Very wrong.

Where was he?

It looked like Raz had left every light in the place blazing. She might be coming back to an empty house, but he'd made sure it wouldn't be a dark one. When she mounted the steps, leaning heavily on her cane, she saw the stain on the cement where Javiero had lain, but most of the blood had been cleaned up.

So had the cookies that Mac had scattered.

"You okay, sugar?" Livvy asked.

"I was just thinking about Mac. He got into your cookies, you know."

"That's what you told me." Livvy had her key out. She used it.

A sudden slap of fear made Sara freeze when Livvy pushed open the door, but there was no one there this time. No waiting killer, no rain of bullets. And no Raz. Sara sighed and followed Livvy inside.

"Well, now," Livvy said, looking around. "I know you're exhausted, but you might want some hot chocolate or tea or something before you go to bed. Why don't you get off your feet and I'll fix you something."

Livvy was so obvious about her curiosity that Sara had to smile. She was obviously looking for Raz, just as Sara was. But he wasn't here. "Livvy," she said, "you are a wonderful friend. But I'm okay. Really. You don't have to stay and fix me things to eat and drink so I won't be alone."

"I suppose that means you don't want me to hang around and tuck you in, either."

She smiled and shook her head. "I don't think—oh, Mac!"

There he lay, a sleepy orange mass of fur on the tweed couch. He did take the trouble to lift his head and blink at her when she said his name. Sara hurried over to him, set her cane down and lowered herself to the couch, happy tears springing to her eyes. "He's okay, Livvy," she said, stroking the cat from stem to stern to assure herself of the fact. "Look, he's really okay."

"He sure is. And he seems glad to be here, too. Didn't even make a bolt for the door this time when it opened."

No, he hadn't, had he? "He saved us twice," Sara said, and rubbed him along the jaw the way he liked best. Mac rewarded her with a rusty purr. "I didn't figure it out until I got to the hospital, but this cat and your cookies were what saved us."

"My cookies?" Livvy looked highly pleased. "How do you get that?"

"I'd made a point of leaving Mac inside because of the approaching storm. Then we got here and your cookies were all over the porch. Mac had gotten into them. I saw him and said something, and Raz understood what was wrong right away. If he hadn't..." She shivered. "But he did. He knew Javiero was in the house."

"I see." Livvy nodded. "He knew someone had gotten into the house, because they'd let Mac out. But what do my cookies have to do with it?"

"You're the only person who has a key other than Raz. If it had been you who accidentally let Mac out, you would have left your cookies inside, not out on the porch. So Raz knew someone had broken in. It had to be Javiero."

"And now Mac is inside again," Livvy said.

"Yes." Raz must have found her cat for her. Now she had to find Raz.

The storm had swept the sky clean. It was a star-studded extravaganza, lush with the light from millions of blazes so distant that the light Raz looked on was ancient long before it arrived here tonight. But the moon was new, a lucent crescent low in the sky, hanging near the unseen line between the restless black ocean and the brilliant black sky. The air was calm and cold.

Raz sat in the damp sand near the ocean and thought about death. And life.

Some police officers made it through their entire careers

without ever firing their guns in the line of duty. Raz wasn't so lucky. Before tonight, he had used his gun three times. He'd shot over the head of a fleeing perp once. The perp had thrown his own gun away and run faster. Years later he'd come upon an armed holdup in progress, and when the gunman attempted to take a teenager hostage, he'd stopped it the only way he could. That time he'd gotten a medal. The gunman had ended up in the hospital, then in prison doing five to ten.

And on the night Marguerite died, he'd killed a man.

A cop wasn't supposed to brood over something like that. He was supposed to regret the necessity and get on with his life. Raz had accomplished only half of that program. The regret. He'd been bogged down in guilt and regret for more than two months now.

But he'd thought the regret was all for Marguerite. Even his body had thought so and punished him accordingly—until recently. Until Sara. Then tonight he'd seen another man go down, with his bullet in the man's chest, and for a moment he'd thought Javiero was dead. Like Jamie Jones. And he'd known that the blood in his dreams belonged to both of them—to Marguerite and her killer.

Lord, he was confused. Why would he be all torn up about scum like Jones? Raz stared out across the ocean and grappled with the images his mind insisted on giving him—images that, in slightly altered form, he'd dreamed about all too often. Images that came to him out of order, in a nonsense sequence of death and regret.

Himself, shoving Marguerite out of the way.

Marguerite, pushing in front of him when her boyfriend pulled his gun.

Jones's gun jumping in his hand, and the huge sound the .357 made in the warehouse.

Two more shots, practically on top of another.

They never did find out what had happened to make the bust fall apart so quickly and completely. Jones might have somehow made Raz for a cop, or maybe he'd decided to keep the money in the suitcase without parting with the drugs.

Maybe he'd found out about Raz and Marguerite. Jamie Jones hadn't bothered to explain why he wanted Raz dead when he pulled his gun.

Raz was alive now because of Marguerite, and because one of the backup officers hidden in the warehouse had fired a split second before Jones got his second shot off. The officer had missed his target, yet the sound of that other, unexpected gun had disturbed Jones's aim. He'd hit Raz in the leg instead of the chest. Raz had gone down, pulling his own weapon as he fell, holding the gun out even as Jones bent and aimed again—

At Marguerite, not Raz. She'd still been alive then. Jones had shot her almost point-blank in the head a split second before Raz's bullet stopped his heart.

How could he regret killing a man like that? Yet it was Jones's blood as well as Marguerite's that had stained the snow in his nightmares for the past two months. He knew that now. Raz stared out at the unquiet sea and the distant blaze of stars and shivered in the cold, predawn air.

The outside chill wasn't enough to numb him. The frozen place inside him had already melted, the snow was gone, and he felt...everything.

He heard Sara before she reached him. "You are one stubborn woman, you know that?" he said without turning around.

"So I've been told." Sara made her way slowly across the sand. She could barely see him, a solid darkness banked against the splendor of the stars. "Javiero was alive when I left the hospital, in serious but stable condition."

He might have nodded. She couldn't tell for sure.

Sara had realized where Raz must be over an hour ago. At first she'd waited, hoping he would come up to the house when he realized she was back. Once she accepted that he wasn't going to do that, she'd put on her sweats and his brother's jacket and come after him. She carried a blanket tucked under the arm that wasn't busy with her cane.

"Here," she said, dropping the folded blanket on the sand

beside him. "Spread that out so we can both sit on it, would you? Bending is uncomfortable for me right now."

"Didn't it occur to you I might have come down here because I wanted to be alone?"

"Of course it did. I just don't care."

He looked up at her then. "Feeling feisty, are you?"

"No. Tired and grouchy." And cold and scared and much too alone, with him gone.

He turned away to face out to sea.

Sara sighed. He wasn't going to help at all, was he? She bent awkwardly to arrange the blanket.

"Oh, hell, give me that before you fall over." He tugged the blanket out of her hands, unfolded it enough for the two of them, stood and scooped her up. Startled, she dropped her cane. He put her down again so quickly she was still blinking stupidly when he sat beside her.

He sure hadn't lingered over touching her...but he had touched her in order to spare her pain. That gave her enough courage to begin. "I suppose that when you work undercover, you get used to thinking of your time alone as safe time. But not everything is best faced alone, Raz."

No response. Well, she'd known he wouldn't make it easy on her. "Thank you for finding Mac."

Still he didn't speak or look at her or...well, she hadn't really thought he would put an arm around her. She'd just *wished.* She'd been wishing for hours and hours that he would hold her, but it wasn't going to happen. Not without some help from her. "I'm in love with you, you know."

"What?" He bolted to his feet. "What's wrong with you? Why did you just say that?"

"I was having trouble getting a conversation going." At least she'd gotten him to react. He was staring at her from a few feet away, his posture saying clearly he was as wary and ready to run as Mac had been when he first started coming around. "Besides, you already knew. We've both been careful not to say it, but you knew. I decided it was better to get it said instead of tiptoeing around the subject constantly."

"Sara." He paused, running his hand over his hair. "Look, you've been under a lot of stress lately. Your emotions have been jerked around all over the place, and—"

"Oh, for goodness' sake! I've been under stress before. It did not make me imagine I'm in love."

"There's a difference between love and great sex."

"Don't confuse my feelings with your own," she said, her voice sharp with hurt.

"Look," he said, and knelt in front of her, his expression hidden by the darkness that lay between them. "You have so much to offer. There are plenty of men who can give you what you should have. Things I can't offer."

Like love? She swallowed hard. "Why did you come down here? Because of Javiero? Or because of Marguerite?"

He shrugged. "Neither. Both."

She took her courage in both hands and asked what she thought he needed to answer. "How did Marguerite die?"

"She was shot." He pushed to his feet. "In the gut, then in the head. Because of me. Jones shot her because of what she felt for me. I don't have any proof of that, but I know it's true." Jerkily he began to pace. "If I'd gotten my gun out a second sooner, she might have lived."

"You shot the man who killed her?"

"Yes, I shot him. I killed him." He stopped several feet away, his back to her. He sounded lost, distant. "Why would that bother me, Sara? Why do I dream about his blood as well as hers?"

She had a huge lump in her throat. At least he'd asked a question she thought she could answer. "I imagine it's like when I lose a patient. It hurts every time. I always question what I did, ask myself what I might have done differently."

"No," he said, and moved a few restless steps. "No, don't try to paint me in your own noble colors. I'm not sorry the bastard is dead. I just…I don't know," he said, his voice rising in frustration. "I don't know what's wrong with me."

"Grief," she said softly. She knew grief too well to mistake its symptoms—denial, anger, guilt—and had wondered if it lay at the heart of Raz's problems. She'd thought his grief might be for Marguerite, but maybe... "Maybe it's yourself you're grieving for, a part of yourself that you lost. Had you ever killed a man before that?"

Sara's words settled inside Raz with all the quiet certainty of the turning of one season into another, one day into the next. Was it that simple? Could it be that simple?

"No," he said, rubbing his face wearily. "No, I'd never killed anyone before. I didn't know...I can't regret pulling the trigger. Even if I didn't shoot in time to save Marguerite, he was fast with that gun. He would have killed me if I hadn't shot first. But I didn't know I would feel so...different... afterward."

"Well, would you rather be the sort of person who didn't feel different after killing someone, no matter how justified the act was?"

She sounded so calm and practical and unfazed. So *Sara*. He turned and walked back to her. He sat down beside her and leaned forward, resting his forearms on his raised knees, and didn't say anything for a very long time. Sara sat beside him, quiet and restful.

"You don't have your knitting," he said at last, thinking of how difficult it was for her to sit completely idle.

When she turned her head to look at him quizzically, he realized the sky had lightened while he had sat there, lost in his internal turnings. He could see her expression now. "No," she said, "but my hands are too cold to do much with the knitting needles, anyway."

He made a disapproving sound and grabbed one of her hands. "Your skin feels like ice."

"That would be because it's cold out here," she said dryly.

He dropped her hand and put his arms around her and pulled her into his lap. She snuggled right in close, and it felt good, so good. For the first time since he'd tackled her and sent them both tumbling off the porch, he began to relax. He stroked her hair slowly, savoring the weight of her, and the soft silk beneath his hand. "Warmer?"

She nodded.

They were facing east, out across the ocean. The sky was dusky now, not black, and the stars were gone along the horizon. "Why did you come down here, Sara?"

"I thought you'd done enough brooding alone."

He smiled. "You consider it better to brood in company?"

"Sometimes." She sighed. "Raz?" Her voice sounded small.

"Yeah?"

"It was my fault Javiero found us, wasn't it? Somehow he traced that phone call I made to my landlord."

His arm tightened around her. "No, it was *not* your fault, and it wasn't the phone call to your landlord that let him track you here."

"Then how did he find me?"

"Tom figured it out after having a little talk with your landlord—who will be doing some jail time soon. He gave Javiero a key to your place as soon as you left Houston. Javiero has been hiding out there." She stiffened and he stroked her hair, knowing she must hate the idea of Javiero in her home, using her things.

"It was the one place we wouldn't be looking for him," Raz continued. "He must have gotten the number here from the caller ID on your phone the first time you called to check your messages, but it took him a while to translate that into a street address." Raz shook his head. "One of us should have warned you not to use the kitchen phone."

"I tell you what—let's toss a coin to see who gets to feel guilty for this one."

He smiled back. "Done." He brushed her hair out of her eyes. "Sara…"

"Mmm-hmm?"

"I'm pretty sure I shouldn't see you when we get back to Houston—"

She sat up. "Are you trying to be noble again? Because if you don't want to see me anymore, I'd rather you just said so. But if it's that you have some misguided notion about doing what's best for me, I...I may have to hurt you."

His hand lingered at the back of her neck. He smiled. "Saint Sara. You couldn't hurt anyone."

She scowled. "I am really sick of you calling me that."

"But it's true. You proved it again tonight when you did everything in your power to save the life of the punk who'd just done his damnedest to kill you. I shot him. You saved him. What does that tell you about the two of us?"

Exasperated, she said, "That was training and instinct, not virtue. Aside from the legal issue—and I was legally obliged to render aid, you know—"

"But you weren't thinking of that when you took care of him."

"No," she admitted, "but it was still mostly training that had me doing the right thing. Just like you did."

"I don't know what kind of bizarre parallel you're drawing between my trying to kill him and your trying to save him—"

"Raz," she said patiently, "I'm talking about the way you yelled 'police' before you fired. It was automatic, what you'd been trained to do. You gave him that once last chance before you pulled the trigger."

He blinked. "I...forgot I did that."

She reached out to stroke his face. "You're a good man, Raz. Not perfect, but good is better than perfect. No one really wants to be around a saint. Saints don't hurt like real people. They don't get tired or lonely or cross, and they certainly don't make mistakes, or get so stupidly self-conscious they can't—"

"Shut up, Sara," he said, and kissed her.

She kissed him back like he was Christmas Day, New Year's and the Fourth of July all rolled into one. She was wrong, but he wasn't going to keep explaining that to her. He needed her too much.

Besides, she might hurt him if he said anything more about her being too good for him. She'd told him so.

The laugh that bellied up from deep inside surprised him as much as it did her. "Oh, Sara," he said, resting his cheek on her hair. "Sara." It was probably best if he stopped kissing her for a minute. His body was getting ideas that it was much too chilly for him to act on here and now. He smiled at the pale peach tinting the sky where it rimmed the ocean. "I'm not letting you go, Sara. I'm not going to be noble or try to do the right thing. What if I gave you some distance, and you took it? No, I can't take that risk. You mean too much to me."

She leaned back to look at him, and her eyes were the same color the ocean was right now, the color of the sky overhead—the chancy blue-gray that hung halfway between dark and dawn. "I do?"

He wanted to kiss her again, for being so pretty and so perfect. "I would have told you earlier, but I didn't know it myself. I've been a little confused." But not anymore. Not since she helped him straighten out some of the tangles in his mind. Not since he'd spent the last hour of the night sitting out in the cold and not feeling it, because all his cold places had been warmed by Sara.

At last he knew the truth. The one truth that mattered. Everything else would sort itself out eventually. "I love you, Sara."

And Sara—shy, uncertain Sara—let out a whoop of delight and struggled to her feet. She pulled him to his feet and demanded that he dance the two-step with her, right there on the beach, with the first colors of the new day breaking over them both.

And he did.

Epilogue

They spent Christmas at the beach house and New Year's at his parents' place. On Valentine's Day he proposed. That, he said, was for tradition.

Raz was dressed for work in a yellow and orange tie-dyed T-shirt, ragged jeans and a bandanna tied across his forehead. The outfit was appropriate for his current assignment, now that he was back on active duty: conducting training sessions on undercover work. Sara was wearing neatly pressed jeans and black lace, and when he handed her the jeweler's box, she was laughing.

Because he didn't exactly *ask* her to marry him. He drove her up to a huge billboard and parked quite illegally in front of it.

The billboard read "Say yes, Sara."
And she did.

* * * * *

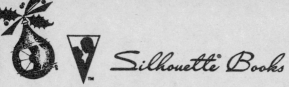

Take 2 bestselling love stories FREE

Plus get a FREE surprise gift!

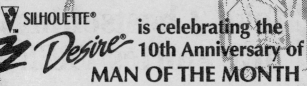
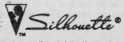

COMING NEXT MONTH

#1189 BELOVED—Diana Palmer
Long, Tall Texans
Beguiling Tira Beck had secretly saved herself for Simon Hart, January's *10th Anniversary Man of the Month.* But this long, tall Texan wouldn't give beautiful Tira the time of day. And she wasn't about to surrender her *nights* to the stubborn-but-irresistible bachelor…unless he became her beloved!

#1190 THE HONOR BOUND GROOM—Jennifer Greene
Fortune's Children: The Brides
His prestigious name was the *only* thing formidable businessman Mac Fortune was offering pregnant, penniless Kelly Sinclair. But once this dutiful groom agreed to honor sweet Kelly, would he love and cherish her, too?

#1191 THE BABY CONSULTANT—Anne Marie Winston
Butler County Brides
Father-by-default Jack Ferris desperately needed instruction in baby-care basics. And Frannie Brooks was every toddler's—and every virile man's—dream. Now, if Jack could only convince the sexy consultant to care for his child…and to help him make a few of their own!

#1192 THE COWBOY'S SEDUCTIVE PROPOSAL—Sara Orwig
A simple "yes" to Jared Whitewolf's outrageous proposal and Faith Kolanko would have her dream: a home *and* a baby. But she wanted a husband, too, not some heartbreaker in a ten-gallon hat. Could a ready-made marriage turn this reckless cowboy into a straight-'n'-narrow spouse and father?

#1193 HART'S BABY—Christy Lockhart
Zach Hart wasn't about to open his ranch to sultry stranger Cassie Morrison just because he and her baby shared a strong family resemblance. He had to beware of fortune seekers…and their adorable, chubby-cheeked children! Then again, what could it hurt if they stayed just *one* night…?

#1194 THE SCANDALOUS HEIRESS—Kathryn Taylor
Was the diner waitress really a long-lost heiress? Clayton Reese had fallen so deeply for the down-to-earth beauty that he wasn't sure if Mikki Finnley was born into denim or diamonds. This lovestruck lone wolf had no choice but to find the truth…and follow his heart wherever it might lead.